THE FOIBLES AND FOLLIES OF MISS GRACE

JEN GEIGLE JOHNSON

To Liz and Cathy

LORDS FOR THE SISTERS OF SUSSEX SERIES

Follow Jen's Newsletter for a free book and to stay up to date on her releases. https://www.subscribepage.com/y8p6z9

TEASER FROM PREVIOUS BOOK

Epilogue from *Pining for Lord Lockhart*

Grace Standish should have been happy about Charity's wedding. She should have been rejoicing with the others. But in truth, she had grown tired of it all, the marriages, the seeking for marriage, the Seasons. With the time finally upon her to have a Season herself, she wanted nothing to do with it.

But Lord Lockhart and Charity were two of the happiest people she'd ever seen. They were perhaps the most suited of all the couples in her family. He not only understood her intelligence and her need to study every sort of topic and discuss it and all its intricacies for hours on end but he reveled in it. She'd never seen a man more proud than he was when Charity bested every man in the room with her knowledge of a particular battle in which Wellington had done some remarkable thing. Grace laughed. She was happy for her sister.

June came to stand beside Grace, her arm going around her shoulder. "And now you're next."

Grace didn't know what to say. Except that she didn't want to be courted. She didn't want to be next. A Season would be asking to get hurt in one way or another. She was just asking to be ruined, forced, or kidnapped. No one talked about it much, but she would never forget how easily she'd been fooled by Lord Kenworthy, how quickly he'd whisked her away and how closely she'd come to being miserable forever.

"Maybe you can choose him for me." Her eyes widened in hope. She knew what June would say. That none of the sisters needed a marriage of convenience, they'd all at last had the opportunity and the means to marry for love, even Lucy who'd chosen to marry their stable hand. But instead of all the typical reassurances she had heard June say before to all their other sisters, she squeezed Grace. "We can if you would like."

And those words, that simple response, had filled Grace with relief. She nodded. "Thank you."

CHAPTER 1

*T*hree could be company. But the lonely part of Grace Standish's heart longed for the even numbers that usually made-up dinner parties: Four or six or most of all, twelve. The eleven that made up the new Standish family, each sister and their husband, was lovely, but everyone knew it wasn't complete. And everyone, Grace included, longed for that nice round number twelve. Everyone was married except for Grace.

In the weeks following Charity's wedding, Grace found herself more restless than usual. She paced, something she'd never done previously. She wandered. Something else she'd not typically engaged in. Walking about on the castle grounds with no purpose whatsoever seemed like a form of escape, though she had nowhere to go and nothing to run away from, that she was aware of.

Dinners were pleasant enough. Morley and June made wonderful companions and more often than not, Kate or Lucy would also join them. They had yet to see Charity and

JEN GEIGLE JOHNSON

Lord Lockhart, but the couple was on their honeymoon, after all.

Tonight was like many others in Grace, June, and Morley's comfortable life together in the castle. The footman called them in to dinner. Morley offered his arm to June and then his other to Grace, and the three entered the dining room together.

The huge table was set only at one end, at their request. The footman held out Grace's chair. Morley held out June's, then the three sat together.

The food was delicious. The French chef had been thinking up new dishes. Tonight, the servants started their meal with soup. It would be many hours before the servants stopped bringing in one thing after another to eat. They ate slowly. They talked. Sometimes they even read passages of their current books to each other.

Tonight, June seemed distracted.

After watching her sister mumble answers and stare into her bowl one too many times, Grace rested a hand on June's arm. "Hello?"

"Hmm?"

"June."

She looked up. "What is it?"

"You're thinking about something."

"Yes, I suppose I am. Aren't we all always thinking something?" She smiled and returned to her soup, but her lip twitched before she placed another spoonful in her mouth.

Grace leaned forward, attempting to catch her gaze anew. "I knew it! What are you thinking?"

June sipped a spoonful of soup. "Can't a person think without an inquisition?"

2

"No, a person cannot." Grace pressed a hand into the table. "What precisely are you thinking? And what has it to do with me?"

June smiled. "There, you see, my thoughts do not always need to pinpoint themselves on you. I do have other cares, you know."

"Of course you do, but if your thoughts were on someone else, you'd tell me straight away. As it is, you won't look me in the face. And you keep mumbling."

June opened her mouth and closed it, then glanced at Morley who simply stared back at her before she, at last, laid her spoon down in her soup. "I've been giving the thought of your marriage considerable attention."

The sensation of cold, then hot racing to her face was the oddest in her life. "My . . . marriage?"

"Yes." June faced her, her eyes earnest. "You did say you wished for an arranged marriage?"

"I do." Grace welcomed the relief that then flooded her thoughts. "Very much."

"May I ask anew, whyever do you want such a thing?" Morley dabbed his mouth and waved for another course of food to be brought.

"I don't wish for a Season. To be courted or 'pretend courted' doesn't suit me at all. I would like the certainty of a man who wishes to be my husband." She nodded as though that would finalize the whole matter. Hopefully Morley would leave it to rest.

He shook his head. "Wouldn't you like to choose the man yourself, to marry for love? We have all the time in the world if that is what's rushing things."

"Not at all." She waved her hand. "I am not in a hurry,

although the thought of things being finalized does bring me a certain amount of happiness." She turned to Morley. "To be truthful, I feel that I will have just as good a chance at happiness if you and June choose my husband as if I chose."

Morley did not look convinced. He dabbed his mouth. "I think we should involve the others."

"Our sisters?"

Morley talked around the footman placing a new plate on the table. "And their husbands if they're willing. We'd have a much greater reach and understanding of the available men."

Grace half nodded before she began to quake about the possible to-do that was about to befall her. Perhaps she'd need to temper their plans before everything enlarged to an overwhelming degree.

June nodded. "I quite agree. Kate and Lucy arrive tomorrow. Charity will naturally get here when she gets here."

"What? They're all coming?" Grace couldn't help the smile that spread across her face, but then she tried to temper its drop when she realized the result of all the Standish sisters attempting to pick a husband for Grace.

"I'm inclined to avoid a big situation. I'd rather it be handled subtly." She looked from Morley to June.

"I'm afraid the invitations have been sent. And if I know the Standish women, there is nothing stopping them from coming posthaste, without great subtlety." Morley laughed. "I do believe we will have a bit of fun, don't you?" He lifted his glass to toast Grace and June.

They likewise lifted their glasses, but Grace could not drink. She wasn't certain what to expect. "This makes me nervous."

"Do not be overly concerned. You will have the last say, so to speak."

"But I don't want a say. I also don't want a large and growing concern among the whole of our family in finding me a husband. I am glad they are coming though. It's been an age since we've seen Lucy."

"Or Kate." June nodded.

Grace grinned. "Oh yes. Do you think she'll have new dress designs?"

"Of course. Although I'm more interested in the little one that's coming early next year."

"Oh, I as well. Just think. Me, an aunt many times over. This is joyous indeed. Who would have thought even one of us would marry when we were all scrimping and saving and cold to the bone in the small cottage off the main road?"

"I knew one of us would marry. But I never in my dreams imagined we all would and be so happily situated." June rested a hand on Grace's arm. "So far. And we shall discover the best manner of happiness for you as well, sister."

"I know you shall. Thank you, June, Morley. I truly don't think I could do this without you."

CHAPTER 2

$\mathcal{M}$ r. Oliver Stewart sat in the shade of his apple tree and pondered the best manner in which to teach the congregation the value of sharing their meager substance with one another, even when so many had so little.

He'd been gifted a lovely vicarage. The view of the ocean rolled out in brilliant shades of blue, unsurpassed anywhere. The Seven Sisters cliffs, rising in white splendor with green sloping tops perfect for picnics and viewing, were also visible from his own humble vicarage.

But so many within his reach were suffering or, at least, had little. There weren't so many tenants as there were servants or tradesmen or shopowners. And without the great estate owners in large abundance, no one was to care for the poor. At least, no one until the Standish women had arrived.

Though in the beginning they were not much more well-off than his poorest family in the congregation, they would arrive with victuals and clothing and cheer to give the suffering families in their parish. And they'd not stopped, even when their castle had the finest in deliveries, the loveliest fabrics, the most beautiful grounds, and from what he'd heard, a greenhouse. They simply shared more now than they had before.

An apple fell from the tree just then and hit him on the noggin like he'd never felt before. "Ouch!" He rubbed his head, looking up into the heavens. Then he took a bite. The Lord provides.

His vicarage had pews for the wealthy. Prince George even had his elevated seat, should he so desire. He had never as yet attended church in the vicarage. He did have his own chapel and clergy at the Royal Pavilion. Besides His Highness and other notable attenders, many of the other estate owners or house owners in town were seasonal visitors.

But Oliver was content assisting those who were truly in need physically, though he'd like to reach the wealthy who often had inner needs that were seldom addressed. He sighed. Back to the problem of sharing. The people had so little. But if they would give, they would receive.

But not everyone could be like the Standish family. He smiled. They were good souls. And each married in turn and moved away except for Lord and Lady Morley and the youngest, Miss Grace. Miss Lucy, however, had married locally. She and her husband had a successful stable right there in Brighton. Which again left Miss Grace. And she was the most active of them all. He'd not seen such a tireless strength.

He tried to shake the distracting thoughts from his mind. The Standish family did not need his help in learning to share. They did so naturally. But Miss Grace's smile lingered in his thoughts. The light that filled her face whenever she smiled could fill a room. She was a woman who knew the goodness of helping others.

At first, she had spent much time assisting with the youngsters at church, but since that time, she'd only grown into a beautiful woman, one he tried not to notice in quite the way he was thinking of her now. He stood. A brisk walk would get his mind back on track.

Of course, there was nothing wrong in courting a woman. One day he would need to. He had felt the loss of having a partner at his side often as he attempted his ministry among his flock. But he was not courting Miss Grace, and it was best not to be thinking of her when he should be doing other things. He had committed to leaving a life of flirtation and the conquest of women behind him.

His walk was indeed brisk. He sent his mind in every direction, looking for that engaging subject to distract him, but he always returned to Miss Grace. His feet switched directions, and before he even had a solid plan in place, he was walking a familiar and well-worn path toward Standish Castle.

What would he do when he got there? He could ask for greater help with donations, but they were the highest contributors already. He could ask for advice from Lord Morley. He was a wise and good man. Perhaps he would do that.

And then there was the obvious looming option he hadn't yet shied away from. He could also simply state that he was there to call on Miss Grace.

His heart pounded within. That seemed rather bold.

What would she think of him, a good five years her senior? He'd always been nothing but a vicar to her. He was certain of that. Although the other day, while providing food for the Kent family, there was a quality to her smile he'd not seen directed at him before.

He shook his head and then stopped in his path. "No. Before I simply boldly declare my intentions, I must first alter the nature of our interactions." He turned and was about to walk the other direction. "Sunday. I will see her Sunday." And flirt with the woman while greeting his congregation? No, that would not do. He turned back toward the castle and forced his feet to move. If anyone could see him now, they would be supremely unimpressed. Was he not supposed to ride in and sweep a woman off her feet? This waffling around on the path leading to her house was embarrassing to say the least.

The sounds of a horse were a welcome interruption to his scattered and racing thoughts. He stepped off the path to let the newcomer pass. The rider seemed to be in a hurry. Oliver stepped farther back, hoping to avoid a kick to the face.

Lord Morley's black stallion turned the bend with the owner himself leaning forward, urging the horse to go faster. But he caught sight of Oliver and pulled back in his seat, the horse battling against him, kicking in the air.

Oliver pressed his back against the tree behind him.

The horse lowered his front legs and snorted, huffed, and danced in place while Lord Morley tipped his hat. "Good day to you, Mr. Stewart."

"And to you. Everything alright this morning, my lord?"

"You are just the man I hoped to see. I'm rushing to fetch

THE FOIBLES AND FOLLIES OF MISS GRACE

the doctor. Lady Morley is having early pains and Grace is doing her best to manage it all, but . . ." He took off his hat and ran a hand through his hair. "I think your influence would be most welcome."

Pleased, Oliver bowed deeply. "It would be my great honor. I was just on my way to pay a visit."

"Oh? Anything amiss?"

"No, no, just a social call."

Lord Morley eyed him for a moment with a hint of curiosity and then replaced his hat. "Excellent. I will ride with much more comfort knowing you are there. Thank you."

"Glad to be of service." Oliver watched as Lord Morley kept the horse at a walk until he was a respectable distance and then he shouted and kicked his heels. The magnificent animal took off, dirt flying everywhere in his path.

Oliver hurried now, his indecision gone and a new energy and purpose lighting his steps until he stood at the Standishs' front door.

The butler ushered him in, and Grace peered down from the stair rails. "Oh, Mr. Stewart! You are most welcome. Have you heard? June is in need of the doctor. Might you join us upstairs?" She waved for him to follow as she turned and hurried away.

He followed, pleased that at least she'd been happy to see him.

Grace rushed into the family's sitting room. As he too entered the room, a smile lit Lady Morley's face. "Oh, Mr. Stewart!" She held out both of her hands but did not rise. "I'm so pleased you've come. How did you know?"

"I happened upon Lord Morley on my way here, in fact.

11

He filled me in on some of the details and asked that I sit with you. I hope that is all right."

"Naturally you are the most desired of all our acquaintances in this moment." She waved at the seat beside her. "For I am in need of your soothing words."

He searched his memory for what he could say during such a time. Bible verses came and went, as did thoughts from his training. But the thing that came to the forefront of his mind was the words to a popular hymn. So he reviewed the lyrics in his head while he got himself situated. Grace had not yet seated herself, and she held up a hand. "Please, I'll only be a moment." And then she rushed from the room.

Lady Morley watched her leave with a small smile. "She is such a dear. I am selfishly happy she is not yet married, for what would I do without her in my confinement?"

"Is she thinking to be married?" The words escaped his lips before he could stop them. What an important question. And one he should not be asking, especially if he hoped to be one to court the lovely Miss Grace. Astounded at his thoughts, he blinked several times, hoping to alter their direction immediately.

But Lady Morley seemed not bothered one bit at his brashness. "It is her time, yes. We will miss her dearly when the arrangements come to fruition."

Her response confused him. Was Grace courting someone already? Were they communicating about a marriage that he knew nothing of? But before he could converse further, Grace returned and took a seat, notebook and quill in hand.

Two pairs of eager eyes turned to him. And he felt a great responsibility descend.

Lady Morley pulled her blanket closer to her. Every now and again, her face pinched and then a worry crossed her brow.

Still unsure of his place, the words to the hymn came more insistent to his mind, and so he decided to begin there.

"We are so grateful for the Standish sisters, for Lord Morley and yourself, Lady Morley, and all the help you have been to our small vicarage." He turned to Miss Grace. "And most especially for your fine sister. She has been"—how would he describe the angelic Miss Grace?—"sent from heaven, quite literally, as those who are in so great need have relied upon her, myself included."

Her face flamed red.

Lady Morley turned a brilliant smile toward her sister. "She is an angel, truly."

He nodded, hardly able to take his eyes from her becoming blushed cheeks and newly sparkling eyes. "So, pleased I am to be able to lift spirits in this moment while we await the doctor. I admit to being overtaken in thought by the beautiful and comforting poetry in our hymns. One comes most specifically to mind. I think I will share the words."

Lady Morley sighed in comfort. "Oh yes, please. I love music. And perhaps Grace could play and sing for us?"

Her face enflamed again, but she nodded. "Of course, sister."

"Are you familiar with the hymn 'Come We that Love the Lord?'"

"I dearly love that hymn." Grace's face lit with the sun from the window as though it has just moved from behind a cloud, and for a moment, Oliver could not look away.

Lady Morley leaned her head back and closed her eyes. "It's true. She played it only yesterday."

"It was on my mind after singing it on Sunday. I'd love to listen to the lyrics again as you speak them."

"Certainly, and then if you would, singing is the greatest balm to any soul, in my mind."

She dipped her head, full of modesty, and he selfishly rejoiced that he would be present to hear her sing.

"I am most drawn to the first and last verses, so I do believe I will share those only." He considered the third and then shook his head. "No, we must hear them all, I'm afraid. They build and are important, each one." He cleared his throat and then began to recite.

Come, we that love the Lord,
And let our joys be known.
Join in a song with sweet accord,
And worship at his throne.

Let those refuse to sing
Who never knew our God,
But servants of the heav'nly King
May speak their joys abroad.

The God who rules on high
And all the earth surveys—
Who rides upon the stormy sky
And calms the roaring seas—

This mighty God is ours,
Our Father and our Love.

He will send down his heav'nly pow'rs
To carry us above.

Grace reached for Lady Morley's hand and studied Oliver's face while he recited the hymn. She was so intent on him that he found himself pouring his heart into the words, sending them straight to her, and her alone; he felt guilty for his shift in focus, as he almost forgot Lady Morley's presence in the room.

When he finished the final words in the last stanza, the room was thick with feeling, and he was hesitant to break the silence. But as he awoke from the dream that held him captive, he knew he must say a few words more.

"I find that hymn highly comforting, most especially in this moment of uncertainty. We are reminded of God's power. The very Being who calmed the seas can calm us here. The God who rules on high can comfort us now. And there is the promise, of course, that His heavenly powers can be sent down." He cleared his throat, feeling sudden emotion as he tried to help these women feel God's love, feel His assistance. "I cannot always promise ease, but I find that I can always promise heavenly help." He looked from one sister to the other. Their shining eyes were gratitude enough.

"Sing it for us, Grace, will you?" June let go of her sister's hand. "The pains are worsening. But this is helping. Thank you." She nodded to Oliver and then placed a hand at her stomach.

"I pray the doctor hurries." Grace stood and wiped her hands down the front of her skirts. "I shall attempt to do the words justice, though I'd just as soon listen to Mr. Stewart's voice." Her face grew red again and he wondered, with the tiniest spark of hope, if her enjoyment and her blushing might transcend a simple spiritual appreciation. Could he be the cause? Perhaps they'd found a way to connect.

She sat at their piano, and at first, her fingers were hesitant and her voice shaky, but as she gave life to the words on the page, she grew in strength and power until Oliver was very much carried away. He closed his own eyes. His heart filled with love and hope, and as he considered the implications of heaven helping on earth, of God's power assisting him in his vicarage, his mind was filled with ideas and thoughts about how that could be and what more he himself could do. So taken with the new creativity that had come, he hardly noticed when she'd stopped.

But the silence jarred him, and he opened his eyes. He blinked twice before clearing his throat. "I apologize. I was so caught up, I found it difficult to stop feeling those blessed thoughts. You have a gift, Miss Grace."

She beamed back. "I do hope I can be of assistance." She turned to Lady Morley and her face was transformed into a mixture of hope and worry in such a way, he wished immediately to alleviate some of it.

"You are most definitely of great assistance." He turned a Lady Morley. "We will do everything we can to ensure the safe arrival of this new child and the health of its mother."

Grace left the piano and rejoined them in their cozy seating arrangement. She lifted a book from the side table. "Perhaps I should read a chapter?" Oliver was secretly pleased that he had another opportunity to listen to Miss Grace from the privacy of his own thoughts, and he knew a book would be entertaining, as well as distracting, something he greatly sought at the moment. He had a work to do for Lady Morley. He had to admit that in Grace's presence, even more than when they were apart, his thoughts were intently focused on her and how he could be seen as something much more than simply her Vicar.

CHAPTER 3

*G*race could not believe the difference in Mr. Stewart. She couldn't put her finger on it, but everything about the man was concentrated—from his expressions and words to the feelings that seemed to flood from his heart. The man was no longer the sweet, passive soul she'd always known—no. He'd become a raging torrent of emotion.

Or had she simply misunderstood his passions earlier?

She couldn't be pondering too much on the intricacies of the vicar's changing personality. June was in a great deal of pain. Grace cringed inwardly every time she saw the flicker of discomfort cross her sister's face. And she knew that this child might begin labor pains in earnest and come too early to their family.

June shifted on the sofa and Grace paused in her reading to adjust the pillows.

"Shall I read?" Mr. Stewart reached for her book.

"Yes, thank you." Grace gratefully handed the book over.

"I stopped at the top of the opposite page."

"Excellent. I must say, when I woke this morning, I had no notion I'd be engrossed in the latest Gothic novel." His mouth twitched.

Was Mr. Stewart teasing her? She eyed him with a new interest. "Who can say, but you might become completely taken with the story. You shall have to return to learn how it ends."

"I quite agree with you and am afraid I am already at its mercy, for I must know if Sir Guthrie comes off conqueror."

She laughed. "And what will he be the conqueror of? Her heart? His sword? The kingdom?"

"I shall venture a guess that he must conquer all."

Grace clucked, thoroughly enjoying this new side to their vicar. "Oh no. He cannot conquer all. Something must be lost. It is the way."

He frowned, a playful sort of look that captivated Grace for a moment. "That is troubling indeed. For I would not wish him to lose anything at this point."

She tapped her chin while June watched the whole conversation. "The kingdom is perhaps not negotiable. He must keep the kingdom."

"True, but what of the sword?" He held his arm out as though holding a sword. "Is that not inextricably connected to the kingdom?"

She wanted to bite back her next words, as they suddenly held much more importance than they ought. "Perhaps, then, his heart? Must he lose his love?" The air felt thick again, as though she could wade through it. Her eyes met Mr. Stewart's. How important was the heart to this man?

He shook his head. "No."

"No?" She breathed out in relief.

"He must not lose in matters of the heart." His gaze seemed to arrest her, pulling her into the depths of his eyes. "In that, he must come off conqueror."

She laughed, trying to shake off this new spell. "The sword, then. He shall have to lose the sword."

"But then he shall be unprotected. What if his fair maiden loses him at the hand of the enemy?"

June held up her hand, and Grace immediately turned to her.

She pointed to the book. "You two will never solve this struggle, for it will go in circles. You must read to discover what the author arranged for our enjoyment."

"Too true. Forgive us." Mr. Stewart sat forward, obediently turning the page to keep reading.

His eyes on Grace sent a shower of awareness that she'd not experienced in quite the same way before. It was as if his very gaze made her more aware of her own self. The hand that held June's, the strand of hair that tickled her cheek, the length of her neck, the set of her ankles. Things she rarely gave any thought to were suddenly at the forefront of her mind.

But his words were soon carried to her mind, and the story took over.

June's breathing became more regular, and Grace didn't dare check, but she suspected her sister might nearly be asleep.

Grace's eyes met Mr. Stewart's. His voice grew softer and more monotone. He winked at Grace but kept reading. She found that watching his face while he read became that much more interesting than even the now-monotone story had been.

The doctor and Morley stepped into the room.

Mr. Stewart stood.

Morley shook his hand and then clapped him on the back. "Thank you. You've been the largest blessing of our day thus far. If you have more to do, you may leave now if you wish."

Grace sucked in her breath. She could not explain herself, but the thought of Mr. Stewart leaving now seemed to take with it all the hope and comfort from their time together.

He glanced in her direction and then back at Morley. "I think I should like to stay if that would be alright."

"Certainly. We would most appreciate your attention."

"Yes, most. Thank you." Grace said the words without thinking first, but she meant them and attempted to keep a bland expression that would assist in the appropriateness of her more emotional outburst.

"I'd be pleased to be of any assistance that I can. Your family has indeed been the best godsend of our vicarage."

Morley nodded but his attention was now completely on June.

Grace stepped away from the sofa and then placed her hand on Mr. Stewart's arm. "Perhaps we can wait in the kitchen?"

The surprise at such a suggestion showed in his rather large and charming smile. "I'd enjoy that."

"So, you are looking forward to some of our chef's delicacies?"

He leaned closer with a conspiratorial eye. "Most

certainly, as you and I well know there is no better faire, except at the Royal Pavilion, and I am not privileged enough to participate there."

"Well, you are most certainly welcome here. And if you ask Jacques Marie, our food is superior to that in the Royal Pavilion." She whispered. "But that stays between us."

"I will keep your secret until I die." He made to lock his mouth with a pretend key, and Grace thought him so utterly charming in that moment, she laughed out loud.

They had almost reached the kitchen when a servant found them. "Excuse me, but Mr. and Mrs. Sullivan have arrived. They are in the front room."

"Oh excellent. Lucy has come." Grace smiled. "This is good news indeed." She turned to the servant. "Could you please send in a tray of whatever Cook has that's warm and delicious, as well as tea?"

"Yes, miss." The servant hurried past them and on to the kitchen.

Grace turned back toward the front of the castle. "This will be even better. I long for news from Lucy."

"I too am looking forward to seeing them."

Grace forced herself to walk at a stately pace, though she longed to run. The relief of another sister to help with June was overpowering. So much so that when she at last entered the front room and pulled Lucy into a hug, tears stung her eyes immediately.

Lucy responded with a lovely clinging hug. "How is June?"

"She's having pain. The doctor is in to see her now. Morley is up there as well."

Lucy nodded. "Good. It's early."

"Yes." They shared a look. Lucy had a certain solidness to her. She was stoic. She followed rules. She knew schedules and kept everyone in line. She was also the only sister to completely break from societal norms and marry precisely who she wished and who was well outside their social circles. And that was just fine with the lot of them.

Her husband Conor was also the most celebrated stable owner in all of Britain at the moment, as the prince could not live without his advice, and many were hoping to breed with his horses. So they were successful indeed.

When the doctor at last descended the stairs with Morley at his side, everyone in the room stood. "What is it?" Grace called out before they were even fully in the room.

Morley smiled. "An early delivery has been diverted."

Grace felt herself melt back into the chair in relief.

"But she is, of course, at greater risk now. We must help her rest and keep her in bed or at least off her feet. We must keep her worries to a minimum. And most of all, make sure she is eating well and sleeping."

"That is much easier said than done, of course." Grace shook her head. "She has so many things planned and people to attend to, and we were just talking of the mini Season here, in Brighton." She hated to bring up her own scheduled items that would add to June's stress.

"Perhaps we can wait on my Season." She looked at those around her. Surely they would see that now was not the time. "I'd hoped to avoid one, at any rate."

"True. " Morley ran a hand through his hair. "We were working on an arrangement of sorts. I have letters out. There is more to be discussed."

Suddenly every eye in the room was on Mr. Stewart.

He stood. "I can see that perhaps my services are no longer the most vital to this group. I am indeed relieved at the good news regarding Lady Morley." He bowed.

But Morley waved him back to his seat. "Oh, stay. You may as well be in the discussion. We are considering Grace and her future marriage. Though she will have a Season of sorts, it is more in an effort to work out the arrangements of a marriage decided upon by her siblings."

"And she wishes for such a thing?"

Grace clenched her hands together, supremely uncomfortable that such a thing would be discussed in front of Mr. Stewart. Must the whole world know her business?

"She does. She's seen all of the rest of us go through our courtships and wants nothing to do with any of it." Lucy laughed. "Though I cannot imagine why, as they were perfectly lovely moments in our lives." She turned to Conor and they smiled, showing a love so deep that Grace felt her stomach lurch. Was she giving up such a love match by hoping for an arrangement?

She cleared her throat and hoped it would also clear her brain. "I just feel that my older and wiser family members will help in this decision. They will see things I cannot." She shrugged.

Mr. Stewart stood unreasonably still. "Your trust is admirable. I am certain as well that they will know best how to assist you. And, might I add, allow your heart to also be consulted." He pulled out a handkerchief to wipe his brow.

"Oh, you've been worried in our behalf!" Lucy rested a hand on his arm. "Do sit. Relax, enjoy Cook's faire." She waved at the new tray that arrived.

Mr. Stewart did place a few items on his plate, but grace doubted very much that he paid attention to a single one.

Grace wasn't certain how she felt about June and Morley having to concern themselves over her marriage while worrying about a child. And the discomfort of their vicar knowing so much about her personal search for happiness was sitting too close to her stomach, causing a heaviness to form there.

Lucy placed a hand over top Grace's. "I think we can take most things off June's to-do list and keep Grace comfortable at all the social events. We can even assist Morley in talking with others about your marriage." Lucy rested a hand atop Grace's.

Grace nodded. "Thank you."

They continued to talk of June. The doctor had left a list of instructions for them all. Morley seemed much relieved by the time he was finished. And as soon as the doctor left, he took himself back upstairs to presumably sit at June's side.

Grace sighed. June had married the best man. For her and for all of them. Bless Gerald, their friend the Duke of Granbury, for the crazy way in which he'd lost a bet and brought Lord Morley into all their lives.

She felt selfish by voicing concerns for her own silly issues with the Season in the midst of the worry over June and her new baby, but the worries were there no matter what she did. She'd been dreading the marriage choice for years, longer than she should have even given it a moment's thought.

The vicar stood. "I do believe that despite the excellent company and food, I must return. I have been pondering a sermon and I cannot manage to formulate just the right manner in which to deliver it."

"I'm certain it will come across just as you intend it to, eventually. You are a gifted and eloquent preacher, Mr. Stewart." Conor nodded to him. "My family often writes of the things you say to us in letters."

"Oh goodness. That is praise indeed. And I thank you." Mr. Stewart stood and bowed to them all.

Grace felt a sudden desire to see him to the door. She almost stood, the words on her lips, before forcing herself to be still. She had no business acting as though the man had come to call on her. Although it had seemed as much. Their looks, their shared conversations, all of it felt very personal, at least to Grace.

He turned as he reached the doorway. "I shall need at least a report on the ending of *Love on the Loche*. Sir Guthrie will haunt my thoughts until I know the outcomes."

Grace approached and laughed. "Most definitely. If you return, we might read together."

He bowed his head. "Then, I shall. Perhaps I might tomorrow? To see about our dear Lady Morley as well."

"Of course, we'd love to have you." Lucy smiled.

But he held Grace's gaze until she nodded. "Thank you."

Then he bowed again and left the room.

She gripped the back of her seat but no one else seemed to notice the air that left the room with Mr. Stewart or the fact that everything seemed far less interesting when he was not there.

She could not explain it exactly, but she did know that she was relieved to learn he would be returning on the morrow.

CHAPTER 4

Oliver stepped with great energy down the lane that led back to his vicarage. He'd spent the good part of his morning with the Morleys, and although he had much to accomplish elsewhere within his flock, he could not regret a single moment.

He was most particularly intrigued with the knowledge regarding Miss Grace and a potential marriage. Was she dreading a traditional courtship to such a large degree? Why was the topic uncomfortable? Many questions lingered from his visit but also many insights. He and Miss Grace had had an entirely different encounter than any before now. She'd smiled and blushed. He'd even attempted a mild flirtation and some humor. And it had come naturally. She was a woman he had enjoyed on countless occasions while doing the work, but to sit in her home, that had been a joy.

Oliver was no stranger to flirting or women or even a kiss or two. Before he'd become a vicar, he'd participated in Seasons and enjoyed women. But things changed with the calling, and he'd struggled to determine the balance between respectability and pursuing his own interests.

He was relieved that June had seemed to pause her child's early delivery. A child born too soon was never a good thing, and he hoped the Standish sisters would be spared such a sorrow. They had endured much, and although they were moving forward with what appeared to be the happiest of lives, he felt it too soon to flood them with the trials that seemed to plague all humans.

One thing was certain. If he wished to get to know Grace in a new way, today was an excellent start, or so he thought.

The vicarage was full when he returned. Some had come to visit and many were in great need. And some were suspiciously there for no reason at all. As soon as he walked in the door, all eyes were on him. Many young ladies and their mothers filled his front room. Was he mistaken or did several eyelashes flutter?

A certain fatigue plagued him in moments such as these.

He spent the better part of the afternoon counseling with families and assisting in other ways as well until he stood from his chair in his study and stretched, feeling as though he hadn't moved from that spot for hours.

And in truth he hadn't, besides to stand and welcome a new visitor to his study. But it was a good work—except for the ladies. He should perhaps be enjoying the attention, but being a Stewart had its challenges, which came in the form of brothers. . . and many lady friends coming to call. He'd had his fill of the simpering hopefuls that spent their lives pining after men, any man, really. These women visiting him that day seemed to be more of the same. Perhaps he was being overly critical.

The good news was he'd figured out the words for his sermon in the midst of all the counseling; they'd come as clear as day.

His housekeeper brought in a large basket. "This has just been delivered from the castle."

"Oh?" He stood.

The basket was full of delicacies from their tea, and it appeared that they had added more for supper too. With the gift, a note was attached. He eagerly opened a half-folded piece of paper. *"You didn't eat nearly enough. Please enjoy, and thank you for your kind presence today."*

He didn't know whose hand penned those words, but it didn't look to be a man's. Perhaps it was Miss Grace. That possibility had him slipping the note into the top drawer of his desk. The housekeeper didn't seem to notice.

"Would you like me to store this in the kitchen?"

"Mrs. Gibbons, that is a fantastic idea. I think I'll just take a bit of this right here. The rest can go to the kitchens to come out at supper and tomorrow's tea."

"Very good."

"And snatch a portion for yourself as well."

"Thank you, Mr. Stewart."

"You are quite welcome. We must enjoy the niceties of life when they come as gifts, mustn't we?"

"Most definitely." She grinned. "Although if you don't mind my saying, you have abundant blessings here."

"Quite right. Perhaps not fancy blessings, but they're abundant."

She nodded like they had the right of it and carried the basket from his study, except for a plate of his favorite tarts from earlier. They were quite good and he'd not miss a particularly fresh batch.

The next day, he dressed with care. The valet was summoned from his other task of caring for the vegetable garden to assist in the dress and care of the vicar. Oliver knew he was odd sending the valet out to the gardens, but the man seemed to enjoy his gardening, and Oliver found that dressing too finely when visiting the poor was only added evidence of their differences. He'd rather focus on their similarities. Also, more often than not he was holding a sick child, working on the roof, or one time, he swept the floors. None of those activities were kind to his clothing.

But today, he was going to begin a new kind of relationship with Miss Grace and he must dress to prove it. He had been rather dashing when he tried in the past and he could be so again.

He wanted Grace to see him differently.

He took his smaller donkey cart to hurry down the lane to the castle, hoping to avoid all dust and mud. When he stepped up to the front door, before he could place a hand on the knocker, Grace opened the door.

"Oh!" She stepped back and then a smile filled her face. "Why, Mr. Stewart. How good of you to come."

He appreciated her glow, the light that always filled her. "Thank you. Did I surprise you just now?"

She glanced inside, then back at him. "You did, but it was the pleasant kind. Have you come to ask about June?"

"I have indeed." He studied her face. "And to discover the fate of our heroine and that man who cannot possibly deserve her, though I hope he rises to the occasion." He laughed at himself and watched her face for a sense of her reaction to his lighthearted ways.

"Oh my. I had no idea it captured your attention so completely. I admit to reading ahead." Her teeth pressed into her lower lip a moment drawing all attention and focus to that singular movement.

"I have some catching up to do it seems." Disappointment clouded his thoughts. "I guess I shall have to borrow the book when you're finished, then."

Grace toyed with her ribbons. "Or if June wishes, we can begin where you left off with her as well and read to her."

He nodded. "If June desires such a thing, then certainly."

For a moment, there was nothing to say. She stood in the doorway, and he stood on the front stoop, a lingering silence filling the space between them.

She rocked back and forth from toe to heel for a moment and then stepped back. "Forgive me. You've come to check on my sister. And I'm keeping you in the doorway."

"No apology necessary. For I came also to see you." The words choked in his throat.

Her eyes widened.

He added, "To read our book?" Then he smiled.

"Yes, I'm sorry. I had no idea, like I said."

How ridiculous of him to think she'd save the story for him. It's not as though he lived there or made regular visits. "No need to apologize at all. Of course Lady Morley and I shall be on the same schedule." He stopped. Lady Morley and he need not have the intimacy of reading a book together. When had he become such a bumbling fool? He might choose this moment to desist talking all together. "It is simply a fun manner in which to distract ourselves from the worries we face, is it not?"

"Most definitely. Which is partly why we are all so indebted to you for your remarkable care. Thank you again for stopping by to see she is well." Had she almost begun to shut the door?

"You are most welcome." They both still stood in the doorway, so he bowed. "Please let the family know I stopped by. And if there is anything else needed from our vicarage, please send word." He turned on his heels and walked down the drive.

He didn't turn back, but he didn't hear the door close. His feet kept moving. At last when he was about to turn out of eyesight, he looked over his shoulder to see a shut door. So that was that. She didn't want a visit from him, only from the vicar. This was not about social calls, not in that way. She'd been clear enough.

He exhaled and tried to put the sting of rejection aside, but it stayed. And he couldn't quite shake it.

CHAPTER 5

*G*race's mouth dropped open while she watched Mr. Stewart turn around and walk away without so much as another word. Had she offended the man? She reviewed the conversation in her mind over and over and could think of nothing untoward. As far as Grace knew, she was about to invite him in to read Gothic novels with her sister.

She walked back into the castle, across the courtyard and into the room with the piano. Something was amiss with Mr. Stewart, and she could not figure out what.

Morley was sitting by the fire.

She stopped in the doorway. "Do you mind if I play the piano?"

"Not at all." He waved her in. "I was just woolgathering anyway. Who was at the door?"

"I believe I've just offended the vicar."

He laughed. "I don't think that's possible. It would be terribly ungodly of him."

She tried to be as lighthearted as Morley. "Too true, and it is absolutely against the man's nature. I didn't used to think he knew how to be offended." She shook her head and sank down onto the piano bench.

Morley's face filled with concern. "But you truly do think he is offended?"

"Well, I can't be certain, but he did just turn from me and walk away as if something were amiss. He asked after June, expressed an interest in our Gothic novel, then simply turned around and walked away."

"There must be more to it than that."

She shrugged. "I've come to play so that I can mull it over."

"I'm baffled. I thought after yesterday . . ." He glanced at her and then shook his head. "Well, never mind. Don't you worry about it. The man does have a bit of an absentmindedness about him. Perhaps he couldn't see how he was coming across."

"I suppose that could be it." She ran her fingers over the keys. "June seems well today."

"She does, though she is going to go absolutely mad if she cannot leave her bed soon."

"Perhaps you could bring her downstairs. Or even outside if she were carried around? If she wishes to see the sunshine."

"Perhaps. For now, the doctor says don't let her leave the room or the bed. But we have hope she can move about more soon."

"We might put my marriage arrangements on hold, then?" Grace didn't know what she hoped for in that regard. One part of her wished to get on with life, to no longer be the third party to June and Morley. But the other part quaked at the idea of beginning a new life with someone she hardly knew. "You will pick a good man, won't you?"

"Of course, the very best." He rotated his head, stretching his neck. Then he turned to face her fully. "Grace, June tells me I must not pester you about this, but I just cannot understand why you would not want to make the decision on your own. Won't you be the very best person to know who you might wish to live with for the rest of your life?"

"When you put it like that, it scares me to death."

"Precisely. Don't you wish to fall so madly in love with a person that you no longer care if it's a wise choice? That it's simply a choice you have to make?"

"That sounds so romantic." She sighed.

"Romantic or daft, they are both the same thing." He laughed. "But don't you wish to be as daft as the rest of us?"

She shook her head. "I've been daft before and not even in love. And it could have been disastrous."

"But you were a child then. That was entirely my fault."

"Oh, it was not."

"It was. I should never have let any of those men near you. I know you would not do such a thing again. You can make a good choice here. Think about it, will you?"

"Of course, but let's move forward because I have thought about it for years. And I feel the most comfortable if you and June and even the others choose for me. I know you won't pick someone you don't all wish to be with." She laughed. "Particularly Charity, though she's not here."

"He will be the best of men. I've already invited a few

prospects down from London to spend some of the Brighton Season here."

She sucked in a breath.

"I figured we could take a look at them close-up, so to speak, and see which we could approach with the prospect of marriage."

Grace tried not to shy away from the very cold and business-sounding manner in which they were discussing her husband. This is what she wanted. And it would be so much safer and easier this way. "What kinds of men are we starting with?"

"Well, June and I and even Gerald and Amelia all thought that since your dowry is healthy and you come from a well-respected family, we could begin with a man of good standing and a title."

She nodded.

"So, we have a marquis, a baron, and the son of a duke coming."

"This is all happening, isn't it?"

"It is indeed. We will meet them all at the ball Saturday, and they're invited to dine with us two days following."

She nodded.

"I'm sorry that we have not been focused more on this the last couple of days. It's just with June and the baby, we have been distracted, but this is happening. The first steps have been taken. We won't forget you."

"If you think we should wait a year—"

"Not at all. Unless you wish to wait. If we cannot find someone you'd like to be with, then, of course, we wait. We have all the time in the world."

A servant stepped into the room.

"Yes, Thomas?"

"Lady Morley is asking for you, my lord."

He stood immediately. "Thank you. I'll go to her at once." He was out of the room without another glance in Grace's direction. It reminded her somewhat of Mr. Stewart's abrupt departure.

Everything about today had her mind swirling in all different directions. The vicar acting strange, men being invited to Brighton to consider as husbands. Men of title. Of influence. And June, about to have a baby.

She began to play the piano, a piece she'd known for many years, one she had played now and again before they had any money at all. Back then, she only played when visiting someone with a pianoforte.

Their days of being poor were more a distant memory for Grace than for the others. But she couldn't feel a drop in the weather now without being reminded of the early-morning chill in her room then when the fire had long since died in the grate and the blankets were too thin to do their job.

She'd missed the piano. As the piece came to life again at the tips of her fingers, she remembered the joy she'd felt in at last finding a moment to play it. Now she could sit and play any time she wished. Did she feel the same joy while at the instrument? Had she lost an appreciation for things that had before mattered most, simply because she now had them always?

She embellished the notes. She'd grown much since those early days. The song was almost too simple.

The vicar lived a good simple life. Did he have a piano? The thought came out of nowhere. But she pondered it. Was he cold in his house? He seemed a happy sort of person, content. He worked. She could not imagine the man idle. And he seemed satisfied. Was he as poor as Grace once was?

Certainly not. He at least knew for certain where his next meal would come from or if he'd have the money for clothes.

He'd been dressed rather fine today. Was he always dressed as a gentleman? She could not picture his typical clothing. She reviewed some of her latest interactions with him. They had been rummaging through Widow Agnes's things in her attic. People came and went, carrying out what was no longer needed. They were covered in dust. She had no idea what he was wearing or what she had been wearing. Clothes were secondary.

She swayed at the piano, moved on to another piece and then another as she considered what she needed to be happy. What if she was poor?

Her smile tugged at her lips. She would never truly be poor. She had a dowry. She had her family. And the castle was always available to any who wanted to live there.

But what if she didn't marry someone of great title or renown?

Again, the vicar's face came to mind. She was not considering Mr. Stewart, precisely. But someone like him? Would that be a good marriage choice for her?

How could she know?

Her breathing picked up as the old familiar fears started to rage through her. The memory of the dark insides of a carriage. Lord Kendall sitting inappropriately close to her, his voice changing from the fun, carefree laugh to a husky, deep sound, one she'd rather never hear again. She could remember the moment when she knew that the carriage was not turning around, not stopping to see the stars or any other promise he'd made, and that she was trapped.

She also remembered the moment when Morley's voice called out in the night. The carriage slowed, and she was taken swiftly and silently back to her own bed and coddled and loved there for days.

That foolishness and the horrors that followed would never leave her.

She'd learned many lessons, the strongest being that a man could pretend to be one thing and then be something entirely different, entirely horrifying, the next moment.

And that was the reason she could never trust herself to make her own choice about her marriage. Surely the others would see through the artifice and choose for her.

She began to calm the more she played, and by the time she'd finished a good long practice, she was feeling at peace again with her choice to be arranged in marriage. She was not yet entirely comfortable with the vicar's strange behavior, but she planned to speak with him on Sunday to see if his odd behavior continued.

And she'd give him a gift of their Gothic novel. She laughed to herself. How utterly charming that their vicar found enjoyment in a Gothic romance.

CHAPTER 6

*O*liver woke up to three of his brothers standing in his front room. He rubbed his face, wishing for a bit of tea before the huge male presence in his house said anything. As if reading his mind, Mrs. Gibbons arrived with the tea tray.

"You are an angel, Mrs. Gibbons, thank you." He turned to his brothers. "To what do I owe this pleasure? Please sit and have some tea."

"We've come to rescue you from yourself." His oldest brother always had thoughts about how to save him. Ironically. Oliver had come to Brighton in the first place, taken on this position as Vicar as an effort to save them all.

"Hmm." He sipped and then drank deeply, wincing as the tea scalded his throat. "And from what are you rescuing me?" His oldest brother helped himself to some tea. The venerable Lord Featherstone was somewhat of a paragon to all who knew him. Not married himself, but as a form of matchmaker, he was certainly the cause of many a union.

His gaze traveled over the three of them. Charles, George, and Jacob. With Oliver, they had made quite a stir their first three years coming out. George and Jacob were twins, and so naturally, they earned attention wherever they went. Then Charles had suddenly taken it upon himself to save the *ton* from themselves. Men approached him now, wishing for assistance in how to woo their women.

"Brother, I am not in need of your kind of saving. Now, if you wish to talk about any other kinds, I have a sermon ready for you right here in my drawer."

Charles shook his head. "No, thank you. We'll listen on Sunday. But of a truth, brother, when is the last time you participated in a social event?"

Victorious, Oliver thanked Lord Morley in his mind. "Just yesterday. I sat with Lady Morley in her confinement and conversed with her younger sister. We read and listened to her play the pianoforte."

Charles had the audacity to yawn. "And a dinner? A ball? Perhaps even a walk in the gardens?"

Oliver stood and walked to the window. "I'm involved in work here—real, hard, meaningful work. It often doesn't leave time for the other pursuits that you feel are so valuable." He turned to face his brothers. "Truly, I'm happy. And none of you are married or thinking of marriage, as far as I can tell."

"Oh, Charles is thinking of it." George coughed.

"But not doing it." Oliver pointed at the three of them. "Leave me be. My home was full of young ladies and their mothers this week. I do not lack for opportunities."

Charles replaced his cup onto the tray. "We're here to

assist. Come, man. Have a dinner to introduce us to the neighborhood."

"And you think that me parading my highly-sought-after brothers in front of the women here is going to help me win someone's hand?"

"Certainly. And it won't harm us either." Charles leaned back in his chair. "Truthfully, I'm here at a friend's request. The least you can do is pretend like we are of use to you."

Oliver shook his head. "We? So George and Jacob are here to push me toward marriage as well?"

"Us?" Jacob laughed. "No. George and I are here to meet some of these women that are purportedly clamoring for you."

"Purportedly?" Oliver's throat tightened, and he strained against his cravat.

"You haven't heard?" George's grin grew in ridiculous amounts. "You're the talk of London, the Handsome Vicar. That's what they call you."

That wasn't so bad. He relaxed.

"The one that can't be won." Jacob downed his tea. "You're a challenge now, did you know?"

Oliver frowned. "I did not know. But that's precisely why I took an assignment with the church."

"Are you certain it wasn't so that you would have enough blunt to live?" Jacob waved for him to sit back down.

"You're a beacon of sunshine today, aren't you?" Oliver returned to his seat.

"We're running low." Charles nodded. "I've taken more clients. So we have enough to get by, but just. It will help if we live here with you, for a time."

"A . . . time?"

"A short time." Charles frowned. "While I'm here I could get you married. And perhaps it's time for me to marry after all. There are dowries to be had, brothers." He raised a victorious hand in the air, belying the unhappiness that was lining his face.

"The paragon himself will marry? What will London say?" Oliver couldn't help but tease his brother, though in reality he had a high amount of respect for the man. When they learned their father had lost most of their financial futures right before he died, Charles had taken his role as the eldest seriously and began immediately in an effort to earn money. And they had done well for themselves. Who would have ever guessed that Charles's gift to help men woo and capture a woman's heart could be a source of income for them all?

It helped that Oliver had been inclined to the church. But the twins were more a drain than a support to the estate. If they at last wished to marry, everyone's lot would be improved. "There are plenty of women here, many with healthy dowries. If you are at last ready to wed, there will be a woman to fill the coffers, so to speak."

"Seems a pity to think of them so." Jacob shrugged.

"There might be an arrangement where I don't feel like I'm using the woman—a match of convenience. She helps me, I help her, and we get along well. That kind of thing." Charles acted as though such a situation would suit him.

Oliver snorted. "And you would be pleased with that arrangement, even after all your talk of love matches and helping the men of the *ton* find their one and only?"

"I would, yes. If it meant we could at last save the estate

and I could stop helping men woo their lady friends." He laughed. "Not that I don't enjoy it. Perhaps I'll keep it on for sport."

Oliver lowered his head in his hands. "Brothers, how did it come to this?"

The room was quiet for a long moment and then Charles spoke softly. "Mother said Father just couldn't help himself. He thought he could save the estate by chance and he kept gambling larger and larger sums until we were left with nothing. He took to drink and died from it."

"There is no reason the lot of us couldn't each make an advantageous marriage. It doesn't all have to fall on you, brother." Oliver thought that certainly the twins could do more in this regard. "Jacob, George, come now, surely you can settle down with a woman of substance."

George snorted. "I don't mind a woman of substance; it's the settling down part. We're young. None of us want to be settling down, not even Charles."

"We'll figure something out." Oliver held a hand out, indicating his home. "The vicarage income is meager. But it is enough for you to stay with me, for a time."

"Thank you. I'll discover if anything can come of this possible wedding arrangement and if not, I'll be out of your hair at least until Christmas." Charles bit into one of Cook's biscuits. "And in the meantime, someone needs to compliment your cook. This is delicious."

Oliver rang for the other servant. "Could you please ready the guest rooms? My brothers will be staying with us." As the servant turned to leave, he added, "And could you send my brother's compliments to Mrs. Rose?"

"Yes, Mr. Stewart." He bowed and turned from the room.

Charles frowned. "Why don't they use your title?"

Oliver sighed. "I'm a vicar, so I'm a Mr. I don't want to be correcting everyone, saying that they are to call me lord all the time. It's a secondary title anyway, a farce. What am I lord of?"

"Father's southern holdings."

"Which consist of a chicken coop, some old, unused mines, and a broken-down shack."

"Nevertheless, it would aid in the marriage department. And as soon as someone arrives from London who knows you, they will call you Lord Stewart." Charles had a point.

"I guess my avoiding society functions has so far kept the title from being well known. I'll consider your advice, thank you."

The brothers separated out to their rooms to refresh themselves, and Oliver hid in his study. As soon as the door was shut, he closed his eyes and began breathing deeply. Charles was here to marry, had discussed an arranged marriage? Oliver then remembered Morley having conversations about marrying off Grace. Morley and Charles could not be talking about the same conversation. Could they?

He hoped not. His heart pounded inside. And it was all he could do to stop his legs from running the distance to the castle, falling at Grace's feet, and declaring himself straight away.

This was ridiculous talk. He didn't have anything to declare. He had seen rather clearly Grace's lack of interest in him as anything other than a spiritual advisor. And he wasn't totally certain he had feelings for the woman. At least, nothing had been explored. Charles would be perfectly in his rights to explore that option. And he'd be an excellent husband.

But Oliver could not stomach it. Not yet. Not without his own chance at wooing her.

CHAPTER 7

Grace was pleased that steps were underway to see to her marriage.

She told herself all morning long just how pleased she was every time she thought of her conversation with Morley. And every time she thought about Mr. Stewart, she felt less pleased. She and Morley would be off to Sunday services in but a few minutes.

She sat at her morning table, looking in the mirror, while Anne placed a few more flowers along her hairline. "Thank you. I felt much like spring this morning, and these were already growing in the greenhouse." The yellow and pink Camellia's highlighted her braid, and she thought she looked rather fetching in a country-vicarage kind of way. She knew what she was doing. She was attempting to impress the vicar.

She did not like the feeling that he was less enthused about her, that she had disappointed him, or that she'd offended him. Perhaps after today she could return to his good graces. It did not do to feel estranged from a man of God.

She sighed.

Lucy peeked in her doorway. "Grace, you look like the angel you are."

"Oh, thank you. You look pretty too." She stood and embraced her sister. "Am I overly concerned about the opinions of others?"

"You? I wouldn't think so. Remember me? I'm the one who was certainly overly concerned."

"You had your very valid reasons to wish to marry well. You were going to save us all." She reached for Lucy's hand and tugged her over to the double chairs by the window. "Has anyone thanked you for that?"

"I'm sure you all have." She waved the thought away. "And haven't the others also done the same, or they would have, were it necessary?"

"True, Kate worked for the papers." Grace laughed. "Did you see her new article on placing flowers in one's hair?" She tipped her head so that Lucy could get a closer look.

"I haven't seen it, no, but if she suggested this look, she is absolutely correct."

Grace nodded. "Thank you."

"I heard some of the men Morley was hoping to meet with are already in town and might be at church this morning."

Grace's face warmed. "Are they?"

"Yes, you are perfectly poised for such conversations to happen. You and I both know they will be getting the best woman of their acquaintance, were Morley to accept them as a possible suitor."

"I don't know about that. But I am grateful smarter people than I are figuring this out."

"Hmm." She squeezed Grace's hands. "Are you ready? Conor and I wish to walk. Would you like to join us?"

Grace peered out the window. "I'd like that. I'll just grab a pelisse."

Soon the happy threesome walked along the dry path toward the church. But shortly after, the path narrowed, and as usual, her married sister walked ahead on the arm of her husband and Grace followed behind, alone. It was time to even out the Standish numbers. It was time for Grace to get married.

They were one of the first families to arrive at church.

Lucy peered inside at a mostly-empty sanctuary. "Oh, let's enjoy the sun for a moment, shall we?"

Grace opened her parasol to protect her face and enjoyed the warmth of the sun on her shoulders. "It's a surprisingly lovely day, is it not?"

Conor grinned at her, his handsome white teeth bright against his more tanned skin. "I especially enjoy this day, standing with two of the loveliest women of my acquaintance."

Grace laughed. "Well, happy I am to be with you. How are the stables? Have you any new foals to visit?"

"We have a new one arriving. You must come this week. I'll send a servant when the time is near."

"Oh, please do! I'd love to see such a thing."

Lines of carriages and phaetons and carts began to arrive.

"Looks as though we've begun our Season, haven't we?" Grace watched the well-known families who came every week to the church give way to the visitors who walked on by as if they owned the very ground they walked upon. "We don't do that, do we?"

Lucy followed her gaze. "Do what?"

Then Conor laughed. "Of course you do. Every wealthy person in England has been taught that they own the ground they walk upon."

Grace nodded. She hadn't always been wealthy, but she always felt she belonged in church. "They should all feel like they have a space. Don't you agree?" She eyed Conor with a glare that allowed no refusal. And he laughed. "You are one determined lass, aren't you? Of course, they all should have a place in the church. I believe our good Mr. Stewart makes certain of that."

"You are correct. For a moment, I felt like Charity, preparing to wage a battle. But surely Mr. Stewart has it all in hand." Her sister who was always changing something had not been back to Brighton for too long. She and her husband would be building orphanages after their honeymoon. Grace laughed. "I certainly don't need to wage anything with you. You are running stables. Charity feeds starving orphans. June and Morley do everything. Kate writes for the newspaper. What do I do?"

"You're Grace." Lucy linked her arm close to her side. "And we all love you for it. Besides, what would this congregation be without you?"

As they made their way toward the door, many of the less wealthy families waved to Grace. The children approached with shy smiles.

Grace paused, greeting and hugging them all. One handed her a small flower.

"What? This is beautiful. Thank you."

The girl giggled and then pointed. "It's from him."

Grace looked over her shoulder at a tall, broad-shouldered man with an open smile. He looked familiar. She couldn't place how she knew him, but she liked him immediately. So she returned his smile, held up the flower, then nodded.

The man was joined by two others, from the looks of them, twins. And then . . . her heart sank. Mr. Stewart. And the likeness was undeniable. She was looking at four incredibly fetching men, all brothers, and her vicar, Mr. Stewart, was one.

Why had she not seen it before? He was probably one of the most handsome men in the *ton*, certainly in Brighton. Of course, today he was dressed in a sharper-fitting jacket, his cravat crisp. His hair was newly cut or styled, and his shoes were shined.

Remarkable that she noticed all of that in a glance.

But the man who'd gifted the flower was watching, and so she turned away, knowing her cheeks were hot red and not knowing what to do about it.

"What is it?" Lucy peered into Grace's face.

"That's Mr. Stewart's brother."

"Is it?" She turned.

Grace groaned. "Now they know we are discussing them."

"I think that was a given. Of course, we are going to discuss them. That was the purpose of the flower."

"I suppose you are correct." She studied its lovely white petals. "How did he find it?"

"One can only guess, but he cared enough to try,

didn't he?"

"Yes, he did." She let it tickle her chin as they walked down the aisle and sat in the second row, the Standish pew. That is what most people called it. But in all accuracy, it belonged to Morley and the castle. Originally—anciently— it belonged to William the Conqueror who then had a daughter who was their ancestor. So, if someone was being technical, it was the Standish pew afterall. She grinned at her nonsense and tried not to wonder who was watching her while she sat there, thinking ridiculous thoughts.

The brothers filed past her and sat in the front row. Of course they would.

Then Mr. Stewart walked to the front.

The music began, and the conductor prepared to lead them in the first hymn. She opened her mouth in surprise. It was the very one he'd read to June, the one Grace had played for him.

Mr. Stewart held her gaze for a moment, long enough that his brothers turned to glance. Then the congregation stood and sang.

Lucy leaned closer and whispered, "What is happening?"

"I don't know."

The man who'd gifted the flower sang out, his beautiful tenor filling the air around them. Lucy raised her eyebrows as though impressed. Conor snorted. And Grace felt something in between the two. Along with a strong desire to run out the back door and hide in her room.

CHAPTER 8

*C*harles had gifted Miss Grace a flower. Oliver's suspicions were confirmed. But he was not going to let his brother swoop in and steal his woman. He choked on his thoughts. Miss Grace was not his woman. And his brother wasn't stealing anything. But Oliver had some history with Miss Grace. He had an advantage here that he was not likely to give up. That advantage might have had something to do with the choice of opening hymn. Should he feel guilty for using his pulpit to impress a woman? Probably, but he didn't care about such things right now. Now he had to combat the flower that Miss Grace was using to caress her face. He had to combat the presence of his overly handsome brothers who were sitting right in front of Miss Grace. And combat he would.

As he stood at the front pulpit, he took a moment—as he always did every Sunday—to look at his congregation. He let his eyes wander from family to family, from person to person. The chapel was filled up again. The Brighton Season was upon them.

But the regular families were also there, albeit somewhat hidden, and he took a moment to see them. And to welcome the new folks.

When he finished, his heart beat a different rhythm. It called him to love—not the love of a woman, but the love of his flock. He opened his mouth, ready to call the world to repentance, to ask them to give, to serve, even in great need. But the words that came out instead were of praise.

He praised the people sitting before him. He called out moments of their love and service for each other. He mentioned Miss Grace over and over but not by name. Would she even know he was talking about her? He daren't look her in the face. But he mentioned the families who were so generous, those who were newly arriving. He praised and loved the people in that room until he couldn't think of another thing to say. Then he praised the Lord, calling out His goodness. He raised his voice to the heavens in love and praise for the One who gave them all.

Oliver had begun work in the church because he enjoyed people. And because he needed an income. But he continued the work because somewhere along the path, he had gained a passion for God. It was this love and exuberance that he tried to share that morning. He felt called to it. And he couldn't withhold the words that poured from him.

The sermon went on. The words flowed. He had no idea of the passage of time or of the people who sat at his front, but eventually, he slowed. The rush of thoughts ebbed, and he again looked into their faces.

What he saw was humbling. Tear-filled faces looked

back into his own. Handkerchiefs were out, eyes were being dabbed. His flock was listening. He was listening.

His gaze moved over to his brothers. Their expressions were varying degrees of proud. That was good. And Grace? She looked away.

The longer he stared, the longer she refused to look at him. He knew he would have to move on or others would notice, so he did.

They sang another of his favorite hymns. He asked for the congregation to remember Lady Morley in their prayers, as well as several of the other families who were struggling.

"And please, remember the collection box on your way out. If you have more to give than is in your pockets, I am always open to receive at the vicarage. We do have a large amount of people suffering at this time, and we will use all collection box monies to help them."

He closed with a prayer, one of heartfelt gratitude for the messages they had all received that day and then he was the first to leave the chapel.

His presence at the door to greet them as they left had been a blessing for him, and it helped those who needed to speak with him have a moment to set up a time to do so.

Many greeted him this time with heartfelt hugs and more tears. In moments like these, he dearly missed a wife, or any form of companion, for he simply could not speak to everyone in the way he'd like. Neither was he equipped with a good manner in which to keep them moving along. At the slow rate they were moving out of the church, everyone would be trapped inside for hours yet.

Then Miss Grace joined him, along with the Standishs and his brothers. And soon, everyone was moving along quite nicely. Grace stood at his side, but she hadn't yet looked at him or spoken to him. They greeted people as they left, one by one. Morley stood across from Oliver. At one point, he heard the words, "Yes, we are taking appointments. He will be free to speak to you at any length you desire this week."

Oliver laughed to himself. They were making up things as they went along. But he was grateful. And he was pleased to have reached the hearts of so many. Hopefully the collection boxes were feeling the additional weight too.

The group stood for what felt like another hour until most everyone had left. When those remaining were at last reasonably out of earshot, Charles exhaled. "My goodness, brother. You've called the whole of Brighton to repentance. You won't have a moment's peace the whole Season. I myself am considering a grand confession." He laughed.

The others joined in, all except Miss Grace.

Oliver turned to her. "Have I offended you, Miss Grace?"

She gasped. "Offended? Not at all. Your sermon was amazing. I feel I have just seen myself for the first time. I listen to you and know of all the ways I should be better, especially these past few days and then at our house. I know I offended you. Those novels—that is hardly godly material. I am so sorry." She held up her purse. "And to think I brought you a copy as a gift." Her eyes filled with tears. "Not offended. It is I who must ask you to forgive my offense." She shook her head and looked away.

Charles snorted but then coughed back whatever amusement he found in the conversation. Oliver felt very much like kicking him.

He leaned closer to Miss Grace. "Might I have a word?"

She nodded and he steered her a short distance away, everyone still standing together, most watching them.

"Miss Grace. You have nothing to feel sorry for on my account. I am neither offended now nor have I ever been offended by you."

Her eyes widened.

"On the contrary, even. You have spurred me on to be better time and again." He held her gaze, hoping she would trust his sincerity.

She nodded slowly.

"And I beg you to please allow me the use of your book." He held a hand out.

Her expression was full of hesitation.

"Please? I found myself awake before dawn, pondering the ending." He winked.

Then she laughed, relief filling her face. "Then, certainly." She reached in her satchel and handed him the book.

"I feel we should join the others. But I wish for so many more conversations with you." He gestured back to the entrance to the church, but before she could speak further on what were obviously closely-held thoughts in front of men who might then tease in fun, he indicated to his brothers. "I would like to introduce you to my brothers." They stepped back to join them.

She looked from him to them. "There is a likeness, isn't there?"

"Yes, we've been told as much." He pointed to Charles. "This is Lord Featherstone. And my two other brothers, Mr. Jacob and George Stewart."

The one called Jacob grinned. "And in case you have not yet met him by his real name, you are standing next to *the*

Lord Stewart among us. As the second son, he got the courtesy title, which he refuses to use. Seems a waste to us Mr.'s." Jacob adjusted his sleeves.

"Oh?" Grace's face colored further. "So we should be calling you Lord Stewart." She curtseyed. "I apologize."

He now wished to add Jacob to his list of those to be kicked. "Please do not apologize. I feel a title makes it difficult to minister to these good people in our vicarage. I prefer to drop it."

Her nod was hesitant but there was a definite gleam of appreciation in her eye. Perhaps even respect. "Well, I can see that. And thank you again for that sermon. I will begin work immediately on all other ways to improve that you suggested."

Had he even suggested that the likes of Miss Grace required improvement? He had meant only to praise her.

Charles stepped forward. "I for one wish for a walk home filled with fresh air and lovely conversation." He held his arm out to Miss Grace. "Would you do me the honor?"

"Oh, well, I . . ."

Morley smiled. "You are all invited to the castle for lunch, so that is the perfect solution to an overused road." He indicated toward the yet unmoving line of carriages exiting the church.

"Of course, then. Yes, a walk would be lovely." Grace glanced toward Lucy and Mr. Sullivan, but they were not looking in her direction.

Oliver could see how she felt somewhat awkward, but he was stuck here a moment longer, dealing with the collections.

Charles patted her hand on his arm. "Come now. You

must show me where all the flowers will begin to pop up along the way." He gestured to the bloom he'd given her. "That was difficult to come by."

"Oh, and it is so lovely. I must know how you found it."

His triumphant gaze did little to assuage Oliver's concern, but at least she would be comfortable.

Oliver nodded to his brothers and then watched as Miss Grace was escorted by the Stewart men from his church toward her home.

Morley remained and watched him with an odd expression. "We will see you at lunch as well, won't we?"

"Oh yes, I'll be along very shortly. And thank you. I would never pass up a meal at the castle with your family."

"I'm pleased to hear it. Grace seems comforted with you at her side." His gaze held Oliver's a moment longer than usual. But Oliver wasn't certain how to respond. "I shall come as soon as I am able. And I do hope for Lady Morley's continued health."

"Yes, she is more frustrated than anything, but she's still doing well."

"Excellent."

Oliver reentered a now empty church and stared up at the stained glass depicting a hill with a cross. His heart warmed anew. He'd never experienced anything quite like that sermon. He could hardly remember what he'd said. He bowed his head. "I thank Thee."

He emptied an extraordinarily full collection box and locked it in the back room before locking the office doors and all other entrances, expect for the main one. He believed in keeping that open all the time. Some level of trust must be placed in the community, and though there was gold to be stolen from the cross at the front, he didn't believe it ever would be.

Miss Grace's reaction to his sermon surprised him and endeared him further to her. She was a golden star among women, and her brother-in-law was working on a smart and good settlement for her in marriage. Oliver's life was simple. He had little to offer. They might not travel or attend the most elite gatherings. He couldn't get the prince to even attend his particular church. He laughed. He might not be what Miss Grace needed, and she obviously didn't see him as anything other than her minister. He shook his head. She was the least among them in need of a serious repentance that she alluded she would begin.

Another thing to consider weighed on him. His brother Charles was considering marriage. That in and of itself said a lot about his situation. If Lord and Lady Morley wished him as a suitor for Grace, then Oliver most certainly should defer to their wishes.

As he stepped down from the church steps and began the short walk to the castle, he knew he had some decisions to make.

CHAPTER 9

$\mathcal{G}$race walked home on the arm of a completely charming man—a lord—and in the company of two other charming men, twins.

All were brothers of her vicar.

As she tripped along on the path, laughing at Lord Featherstone's endless quips, she could not reconcile her life.

"Tell me, Lord Featherstone, what brings you to Brighton?"

His eyes widened a moment and then he looked back over his shoulder. "Here to pay a visit to my brother and visit old friends. Lord Morley invited me."

Her heart did a double beat. Morley's invitation. She considered her flower. The walk. His attentiveness. So, he was here to consider an arranged marriage . . . with her.

"Are you well, Miss Grace?" He leaned closer, peering down into her face. His expression was full of understanding, perhaps too much.

"Oh yes. I am well. My mind is full right now, that is all."

"My brother's sermon." He whistled.

Jacob laughed. "Some vicars might just read Psalms and keep everyone happy."

"Oh, but Oliver is not like some vicars." George shook his head. "The man can never simply do anything lightly. It must be the most well-thought-out and remarkable version of the thing."

She tilted her head, attempting to reconcile their thoughts with the humble and simple man she thought she knew. "He doesn't appear to wish for accolades."

"The man won't even take a title." George grunted. "No, he just simply never does anything with half a heart. That's probably a better way to describe him."

She nodded.

"You seemed particularly moved by his words." Lord Featherstone looked to the heavens. "I admit to being touched as well."

"He's never been quite so moving before." She shook her head. "It was as if his words were directed at me."

"Or me." Lord Featherstone rested his other hand over hers. "Do not take them too closely to heart, as he quite likely did have me in mind as he spoke."

"The lot of us." Jacob agreed.

"Why do you think so?" Grace was newly curious about their relationships as brothers.

"Well, most simply because he's outdone himself on the one Sunday we are here in town."

"Will you be staying just the one week?" She wished they would stay, or at least she thought she did.

"Oh no, who's to say? I think we might pass the Season in Brighton."

"I'm pleased to hear that. I'd greatly enjoy your company, as would most of Brighton." She smiled and recognized the sincerity of her words. The brothers were jolly, attentive, and perhaps being considered by Morley as possible suitors.

"Tell me what interests you." She directed her question at Lord Featherstone.

He dipped his head. "I am a studier of persons."

She turned more fully to him. "Are you? That's intriguing. What do you discover about them?"

"Oh, I don't know. But take you, for example."

"Me?" Her cheeks warmed, whether from embarrassment or pleasure, she could not say. But she turned all her attention to this intriguing new lord. "In your knowledge of studying people, what have you learned of me?"

"You are incredibly humble and sincere."

Somewhat disappointed, she nodded. "I can see that."

"But those two qualities do not entirely hide a healthy dose of the precocious."

"What?" She laughed. *Precocious.*

"And the daring. I suspect you are a daring lass who wishes for a bit of adventure."

She turned away, his assessments coming too close to qualities she'd like to hide.

"Am I correct?" He tilted his head so that she would have to turn to him.

"Yes, too correct if you must know."

He laughed with victory. "I knew it."

"Well, so what if I am? There is no adventure to be had, so those things must be ignored, mustn't they?"

"Oh, I don't know about that." His face suddenly filled with riddles, and she at once wished to solve them all. "But we shall have to give that some thought, won't we? Now tell me, who will be dining with us?"

They were approaching the castle at this point. She looked high up to its closest turret. "I don't really know for certain. But you can plan on Mr. and Mrs. Sullivan, perhaps Lord and Lady Dennison, Lord Morley. Unfortunately, my sister is to her room in her confinement."

"I'm sorry to hear that. Perhaps we can do something to alleviate her boredom."

"Perhaps. I'm certain any efforts in that regard would be much appreciated."

"Excellent. George is our much-celebrated jester."

George snorted again. "Why must I be the brunt of all your humor? I assure you, Miss Grace, I am a serious fellow with an excellent mind who wishes only to be appreciated."

She found herself laughing with the others. "I'm certain you are."

They walked around to the front so that she might invite them in through the grandest entrance. As they stepped into the front hall and she walked with them out into the courtyard, she was not disappointed by their reactions.

"What a remarkable home. You say you won this in a game of cards?" Lord Featherstone shook his head, turning in a circle to get all the views.

She smiled. "Our dear Morley did. He was strapped with the lot of us as poor tenants in the winning."

"Fortunate for him, I'd say." Lord Featherstone tugged

Grace's hand with him as he began a walk. "Might we have a short tour before the others arrive?"

"Of course." She waved to the other brothers. "Come, I feel we are ignoring you."

"Yes, thank you. Nice to be noticed." Jacob moved to Lord Featherstone's side.

"Oh tosh. As if the two of you are ever ignored." Lord Featherstone raised his eyebrows. "Don't concern yourself one moment for them in that regard. Just watch how Brighton will come alive with talk of the Stewart twins."

She could very well imagine such a thing. "I'm certain I'll hear tales of all three of you."

"Unless others of us are more singularly focused." His eyes found hers, and she was again reminded of a possible arrangement.

"Yes." She turned away. "Now, this hallway is one of particular mention."

Lord Featherstone said all the right things, did all the right things, and certainly was a handsome enough man. But she panicked whenever she tried to consider him as anything besides just himself—a nice man. If she thought of him as a potential husband, her mind started racing with all the possibilities of him being a truly abhorrent person just pretending to be upstanding. She doubted everything she thought and therefore him. These thoughts of hers were old friends. He and his brothers did not deserve such opinions from her.

So she led them on a most descriptive tour.

"This hallway is where we found the jewels." She wiggled her eyebrows in such an exaggerated manner that they all laughed.

"Oh, do tell." George grinned.

"You know that when we first acquired the place, it was falling apart?"

"Yes, everyone is grateful you have mended the terrible eyesore of Brighton. Instead of ruins, we have a lovely castle."

"Too true. This hallway was one such location. Right about here." She stopped and pointed to some newer-looking stone. "The walls had crumbled, and we stood outside."

"Remarkable." Lord Featherstone ran his fingers along the wall. "The repair is superb.""I agree. We can thank His Grace, the Duke of Granbury for that. And, of course, Lord Morley.""A remarkable family in remarkable circum-stances." Lord Featherstone continued their walk down the hall. "And all these extra rooms?"

"Oh, those are most excellent for a boring afternoon. There are boxes in there of ancient origin we have still not opened. Crates. The last time we looked, we found a remark-able family tree that included Kates's husband."

Lord Morley joined them in that moment. "I've been looking for you, and I'm so glad you've arrived. I believe the other Mr. Stewart has also joined us. Shall we?" He indicated that they return down the hall.

Grace was relieved for yet another distraction from the thoughts that plagued her. As much as she tried, Lord Featherstone was more a potential husband than simply a man of her acquaintance, and that made her thoughts a whirling maelstrom.

The table was laid in typical castle style, with all the niceties decorated in the loveliest manner. Lord Morley must've requested the extra details, as June was still in bed.

Grace knew the minute Mr.—Lord—Stewart entered, even before the servants announced him. She tried not to stare or even let on that she noticed, but she was so extraordinarily self-conscious, she was certain it was obvious to all. Morley kept him busy on the other side of the room. They discussed something with great hilarity and she inched toward them. But before she arrived, dinner was called.

Lord Stewart turned to her. He knew right where she was. He held out his arm. "Might I escort you in to lunch?"

She nodded. "Of course." The hand she placed at his elbow trembled slightly. "I'm glad you've come."

"I as well. It was easy enough to close up the office. And I came as soon as I could."

"You are missed when you aren't here." She swallowed. Did she sound overly needy? Or personal? He was her vicar. He was not Lord Featherstone, even though knowing them as brothers brought a new sense of familiarity with Lord Stewart that she'd not felt before. She couldn't be flirting with him. And she really couldn't tell if she was flirting. Or perhaps being friendly. She bit back a sigh.

His eyes lit with pleasure. "I am so pleased to be thought of, missed even."

"Very much so." She lowered her lashes.

"I feel the same."

Her heart pounded in wonder at his words. But before she could consider his meaning, Morley waved at them to find their seats.

Grace sat next to Lord Stewart, much to her equal parts pleasure and consternation. What she really needed was several hours in the library to contemplate his sermon and to figure out how to speak to the man.

Lord Featherstone sat across from her. Once they'd all been served the first course, he lifted his cup. "Might we make a toast?"

Everyone raised their glass. Morley, with the biggest grin of all, asked, "To what or whom are we toasting?"

Lord Featherstone faced Lord Stewart. "To my brother, the man who continually surprises us all."

"And to my brother," Lord Stewart chimed in, "another man who is full of surprises."

Grace looked from brother to brother, and when her gaze fell on Lord Morley, she was surprised to see the slightest wink he sent in her direction.

Lord Morley continued, "And to my dear wife, Lady Morley, in the hopes that the newest Morley will arrive safe and sound when he is due." Everyone raised their cups higher and called out, "Cheers."

Lord Featherstone and Lord Stewart seemed to be having some sort of silent conversation across the table with one another.

Lucy sat at Grace's other side. She took a sip of her soup and then said, "I hear there's to be a ball."

Conor chimed in. "Not just any ball. One hosted by the prince regent himself at the Royal Pavilion." He grinned. "I never tire of balls."

"It's because you only just began attending in earnest." Lucy's tender teasing was heart warming. "You haven't yet had your fill."

Conor raised his cup. "And everyone there wants to buy a horse."

Lucy laughed, and Morley raised his glass again. "Too true. You've been wonderfully successful."

"Thank you, Morley."

Morley nodded. "In my mind, a ball is an excellent way to start off the Season. If someone is in town, they will be there. And certainly, more will be drawn to our area from London as the news spreads."

"I've never seen you so involved in a Season before." Lucy shook her head.

"It's all due to our Grace here; this will be her first official coming out."

"And hopefully my last." She kept her eyes turned down. Her idea of having a marriage arranged in her behalf was turning out to be more awkward than she anticipated. Would they speak openly about her coming out in front of a man to whom she might be arranged? She did not know how these things were done. And the presence of Lord Stewart at her side only served to muddle things in her mind.

"The Season is brilliant and full of fun. I'm sure you'll enjoy it immensely." Lord Featherstone grinned. "It's especially enjoyable for one who longs for adventure."

"Is it? And how so?" She'd not considered his adventure assessment of her before. A part of her knew he was right, but a part of her suspected there was more he'd never really understand about her.

He rubbed his hands together. "There are just so many new faces to know and meet, as well as parties to attend. I imagine someone such as you would revel in the Season, were you to allow yourself to enjoy it." He sipped from his cup, watching her with great amusement.

Lord Stewart leaned closer to her. She was so confused in regard to him. Who was this new man who gave a sermon that might change her possibly forever, who also suddenly appeared so handsome, and who was in actuality a lord? And marriageable? She couldn't believe the thoughts that flashed through her mind. He leaned even closer to her, the air between them heating just the slightest amount, and asked, "Are you one who longs for adventure?"

"I . . ." She glanced at Lord Featherstone who seemed highly amused by the direction of the conversation. "I don't know."

Lord Stewart took her hand in his, her bare skin tingling immediately from his attention. "People can find adventure in all manner of places."

Her hand hummed from his touch, and for a moment, all the words she might have said left her brain. She cleared her throat. His thumb moved along her bare skin in the briefest caress. Her eyes widened and he smiled. She tugged her hand back, knowing that she'd never be able to formulate another thought if she didn't. "That is true. I've found a lot of adventure here in this castle. There are still crates of artifacts to explore, in fact." She lifted her chin in an almost unexplainable challenge to Lord Featherstone.

"Too true. I would be delighted to go on that adventure with you." Lord Featherstone dipped a spoon in his soup. "And no doubt there are others the Season will offer."

Lord Stewart looked from Grace to his brother and back and seemed to shift in his seat farther from her. "My brother is the one in our family most inclined for adventure."

Her hand shook as she brought the next spoonful of soup to her mouth. "Is that so?"

"Yes. He's also the most able to offer stability. Quite a good catch for the Season, if I were to choose, stable and adventurous." He nodded more times than was necessary and then seemed to ignore them all while he focused on his soup.

Grace was at a loss to understand precisely what was going on at her end of the table. She raised helpless eyes to Lucy.

Her sister grinned. "Shall we tell the stories of our first Seasons?"

Conor shook his head. "That's hardly fair, as I didn't have one."

"Oh, you certainly did. You were the talk of London."

"Among the men." He snorted. "Thankfully, one woman had already seen me." He lifted a glass to his wife who clinked hers to his in response.

They turned to Morley who nodded. "I wish Lady Morley was here to add her better part of the story, but we were a match from the beginning."

Grace and Lucy laughed.

Morley looked from one to the other of the sisters. "Except for that other man who we had to be rid of first." He cleared his throat. "And except for the fact that she was uncomfortable being beholden to me. But that was cleared up before we knew it, and she stopped resisting what we both knew."

"And what was that?" Grace leaned closer. She'd never heard Morley's perspective on the happenings of his and June's courtship before.

"That we were well-nigh in love with each other from the start."

Grace nodded. She wasn't certain June thought she was in love with Morley from the start, but Grace had certainly seen that they were a good match from the very beginning.

This was all excellent for them, but she remembered all those nights of not knowing if they would ever be together, the frustration and hurt June felt when she wasn't certain about Morley, when she didn't want him simply doing his duty by her. Nothing about it was easy or even fun. Could Grace skip all of that if someone simply arranged it all?

As she watched Lord Featherstone, the brothers, and felt an almost brooding presence of Lord Stewart beside her, she wasn't certain a person could ever skip some of those emotions. Would she have to get to know her husband after they were married? Would she be plagued with the same insecurities if she fell in love with him? Wonder if he loved her, to second-guess his actions, to be unsure of herself?

She wanted to lower her forehead into her hands and hide from it all.

Today had been a day full of things to think about, and she was surrounded by people. She longed for the quiet of her room. There was simply too much going on in her mind, too many questions, and no answers.

Lord Stewart leaned close again. "Perhaps we could simply discuss the weather?" His eyes were sincere, and hidden somewhere in their depths was the slightest sparkle of humor.

She breathed out in relief. "The weather is far less complicated than what I have going on in my head right now."

He nodded, then he called out to the table. "I have heard

that they have predicted a very cold winter much like our last but with more snow."

"Snow!" Lucy shivered, and immediately reclamations carried around the table. Everyone began discussing where they were and how long the cold had lasted during the longest spell of winter England had known.

She felt her shoulders relax, and she lifted another bite of warm soup into her mouth. As the conversation continued around in great animated tones, she allowed her mind to contemplate other quieter things.

The grateful eyes she lifted to Lord Stewart were met with an appreciative response, almost tender. She studied him for a long moment before returning to her food, much calmer than before.

Lord Stewart was so much more than she'd ever considered.

Much more indeed.

CHAPTER 10

O liver joined the men in a game of billiards while Lucy and Grace went upstairs to spend time with June after dinner. Charles was already chalking up his stick. The balls were set in their triangle formation.

Morley handed Oliver a stick. "We will be next."

"Excellent. Thank you."

Morley stepped farther away from the table, back into a corner. "Might I have a word with the vicar?"

Oliver stood up straighter and approached him. "Certainly. Is everything all right with Lady Morley?"

"Oh yes, she is as well as can be expected, thank you. I am thinking more of Grace right now."

Oliver cleared his throat. "Oh?"

"Yes, I must make a decision in her behalf. And I don't feel up to the task. How can a man determine what would be the happiest decision for another? How am I to know who she should marry?"

"You are in quite the predicament. I do not know how fathers do it, let alone brothers-in-law."

"And I've been a sort of father for her, but more like an uncle, or perhaps simply a brother. Whatever I've been, I'm all she has in that regard. I and the other brothers-in-law, and Gerald, His Grace, of course."

"Of course." Oliver waited, feeling uncomfortable with his own feelings for Miss Grace in relation to this conversation. But more must be coming.

"I wonder if I might ask for your assistance."

"Certainly."

"I wish to encourage Grace to, er, choose for herself." He searched Oliver's face as though looking for a response of approval that he needed.

So far, this task seemed one Oliver would most happily embark on. "I do think that would be the best course, but would she? If I may, why is she so set on you choosing?"

"I feel I'm not one to share her history, but for reasons known to her, she feels inadequate in her judgement of human nature. And she thinks the whole process of falling in love and choosing a spouse to be fraught with trouble and worry and challenge. She's had four sisters marry, I'm afraid." His grin was wry.

"She's not wrong, is she? Do we know anyone who simply just falls in love and marries, simple as that?"

"Not too many, I'm afraid. And it will always seem easier to those of us not close to the situation. She was unavoidably, intimately aware of all the details of everyone's courtships."

Oliver nodded. "And now she wishes to have none of that excitement for herself?"

"Precisely, as well as doubting her own ability." Lord Morley faced him, his back to the room. Charles watched them both. Oliver wouldn't be surprised if the man had telepathic powers.

Oliver put a hand in his pocket. "Have you spoken with her about your desires?"

"Not yet. I hope to do so this evening. But watching her with you, seeing how she responds so well to your suggestions, gives me leave to feel that perhaps you could be a part of the conversation—"

His breath caught in his throat. "Pardon me?"

"Join me in the study when I attempt to encourage her to choose for herself."

Oliver was shaking his head before Morley finished his sentence. "I don't think I'm the person she wants in there when you have such a personal conversation."

"But she trusts you. You're an advisor to her. You saw how she responded to your sermon. If you were to even tell her you thought it best . . ."

Oliver did not like the sound of this. He did not want to be a part of the conversation, and certainly did not wish to be seen as that sort of an advisor to Miss Grace.

Charles called over. "I'm unsure what your conversation entails, but I did hear the word advisor, and I must say, my Oliver is the best in that regard."

Oliver narrowed his eyes. What was Charles up to? He himself was considered one of the most sought-after advisors in all of London as far as love was concerned, although, of course, Morley likely didn't know that.

"It's settled, then. Join us, at least for the conversation."

Oliver wasn't sure how to decline the request. He was

their vicar. Advising and counseling were part of his assignment. The Standishes were his largest donors and a dear
family. "Certainly. I will do my best."

"Capital." Morley gripped Oliver's shoulder. "My thanks
to you. Especially with June so unavailable, I am counting
on friends."

They both turned to watch Charles sink his last ball.
"Excellent game, George. We'll have to play again."

"Hmm. Yes." George replaced his stick and moved to the
port container, pouring himself a cup.

The men exited the room just as Grace and Lucy were
coming down the stairs. Oliver couldn't help himself; he
watched Miss Grace and admired her every step. She was
full of light and energy, and her smiles filled the whole
room. They filled his heart with expectant hope. She was
someone he most dearly wished to know better, to court, to
explore a possible relationship.

Morley stepped into his line of sight, blocking his view.
"Come, Grace, I'd love to have a word, and I've asked our
noble vicar to join us."

Charles didn't even hold back. He laughed. And when
everyone turned to him, he simply held up his hands. "I
apologize. George is overly amusing tonight."

George shook his head. "Always the jester to you."

"Although, I was hoping for a walk with Miss Grace this
evening, if I might," Charles called out.

"Certainly, we will only be a moment." Morley nodded.
With a hand at Miss Grace's back and a wave to Oliver,
Morley led them both back down a side hall and into his
study.

He indicated they sit in a small seating area near a fire

that had been recently stoked. Oliver admired the staff at the castle. How would it be to have so many servants?

He would not be able to provide such a life for Miss Grace, a life she'd grown accustomed to. Even with more money, his vicarage was small. It couldn't staff more people. And by nature, he attempted to need less than a typical noble.

Perhaps helping her find and choose a man who could offer her the world was for the best.

Morley reached for Miss Grace's hand. "I am so sorry for the surprise visit of Lord Featherstone. As I'm certain you have guessed, he is one of the men I had asked to come so that we might make a marriage choice for you."

She sucked in a breath and glanced in Oliver's direction. "Morley. Why are we having this conversation with Lord Stewart here?"

"I asked him to come. He is such a valued advisor. He is a good man. And he seems to counsel us in wise ways every time we ask."

She nodded but seemed far from comfortable.

Oliver stepped closer, one hand out. "I do not have to stay."

"Please do. Tell him, Grace, we trust him completely."

She glanced at Oliver for a moment with hesitancy but then nodded. "Of course, we trust him."

"That's all we need, then. So, Lord Featherstone is one of three men I've asked to come. And I think we can all agree he is most excellent. An admirable prospect in every regard."

"He is. I quite like him as well. He's amiable and fun and good."

"Remarkable. Have we found a good one with our first attempt?" Morley sat back in huge relief.

"Wait, I don't know." Grace held up her hand at the same time Oliver leaned forward to speak.

Oliver breathed out in relief and nodded for her to continue.

She clenched her hands together in her lap. "If you're asking me, please don't. I cannot have this responsibility on my shoulders. I don't know anything about him."

Morley ran a hand through his hair. "Well, neither do I. Grace, please, engage in this decision."

She started breathing faster, and Oliver saw in her some real fear. He reached out a hand and placed it over hers as it now gripped the side arm of her chair. Her fingers relaxed under his.

"Please, Miss Grace. What is it?"

"I've said it so many times. There's nothing else to say but that I cannot make this decision."

"I understand." Oliver applied pressure to her hand.

"You do?"

"Certainly. Perhaps what we need here is simply more time."

She opened her mouth in what looked like disagreement.

"I'm not saying time for *you* to decide. Just time to grow accustomed to the plan. Meet the men. Let Lord Morley investigate and work out the details over *time*. You might grow accustomed to them as friends. And with time, a decision could be made. Perhaps you might even feel up to contributing your thoughts, your reactions to the men, your inclinations." He held her gaze, trying to infuse her with confidence and hope. She was indeed not ready to make this kind of decision.

"Perhaps. But also, I'm tired of being alone. I don't wish to be the third person in every conversation, to be the only one without someone always on my side, to not have another to team up with."

Morley raised a finger. "Team with Lord Stewart."

Oliver sucked in a breath and turned to Lord Morley.

He and Grace both responded together. "What?"

"Certainly. I'm surprised I didn't think of it before. Who better than our vicar to advise us? With June in a troubling situation, my mind is in multiple places. While we attempt to work through our best options, use whatever time you need, focus on enjoying your Season and use Lord Stewart as one to counsel with. I'm certain that between the two of you, Grace will feel more comfortable with the whole plan."

Oliver frowned. "But Lord Featherstone is my brother. I don't see how—"

"That's neither here nor there. I'm not asking you to choose her husband for her. Simply assist her in feeling good about her husband. I'll choose the man."

Oliver had nothing to say that would be palatable in their ears at the moment. He turned to Miss Grace, an apology on his lips, but what he saw there stunned him.

Soft, warm eyes full of gratitude stared back into his. "Would you do that? I feel so much more comfortable with a sounding board, someone to talk these things through with. Perhaps it might be a little awkward at first. I've never discussed my potential marriage with a man of the church before, but I do appreciate this oh so much." She smiled a wavery smile and looked on the verge of tears. Hopefully they were tears of relief. But Oliver felt nothing akin to relief. No matter his feelings, however, he choked out his response. "I would be happy to help."

"Excellent." Morley placed his hands down on the table. "You'll be attending Prinny's ball, no doubt."

"I will, it seems."

"The other men will not have arrived by then. So it will just be a continued acquaintance with Lord Featherstone, and honestly with any others she might fancy at the ball. Who knows what could happen during a waltz, after all. I've found them to be quite effective." Morley chuckled to himself, then stood. "We should return to the others. Didn't Lord Featherstone request a walk?" He winked. "I must admit, with your help, Lord Stewart, I'm feeling much more relieved by the whole thing, don't you agree, Grace?"

"I do, thank you." She smiled one more grateful smile at Oliver and then skipped out of the room. He fell back into his chair.

Morley was ready to make his way out. "Did you need to talk about something more?"

"No, please don't mind me." Oliver stood. "I was... wool-gathering."

"Of course. You must have so much on your mind, an entire congregation to care for." Morley clapped him on the shoulder. "Thank you again. You are the best man for this job. I can see it already."

"I'm sorry so much falls to your shoulders. With any luck, Lady Morley will be well and you will soon have a new child delivered."

"With any luck and not too soon, mind. At the right time."

"Yes, I will pray for you all."

"Thank you."

Morley and Oliver made their way back down the hall and joined the party. Grace and Lord Featherstone were nowhere to be seen, but Lucy and her husband were also missing from the group.

Morley brought out cards for whist. "Next dinner party will not be so quickly thrown together. We will have even numbers and all the things June would have helped me plan. In the meantime, gentlemen, how about a game of whist?"

As he dealt the cards, Oliver could not keep his mind from the walk outdoors or from his new assignment or from his own desire to perhaps have his own moment with Miss Grace, her hand on his arm, looking up into his face. Would he ever change her expression from one of piety and respect to admiration and love? Could he incite in her a desire to embrace or even kiss him? He wanted to shake the thoughts from his mind, but they came rushing in along with everything else. Perhaps as the vicar he was not supposed to think about kissing a woman, but with someone as special as Grace—in the right moment, as an expression of their shared love—he could not think of anything closer to God than that.

Forgive him, but he could not.

CHAPTER 11

*G*race enjoyed her walk with Lord Featherstone. He was attentive and close and flirted with her in a terribly enticing manner. They'd been walking for a long time; Grace knew they should get back. Lucy and Conor had joined them but kept their distance.

Lord Featherstone had found the castle's greenhouse where they both admired the vegetables. "Forgive me. I know we must return. Mr. and Mrs. Sullivan are no doubt tired of the greens. But I think I might enjoy anything with you at my side. It is rare, but with you, I feel I've found the soul who could make the mundane seem not so."

"Do you find the greenhouse mundane?"

For the first time since she'd known him, she saw a hint of fluster in Lord Featherstone.

"Of course not, no. It's rather engaging, is it not?"

She laughed. "Engaging? Hmm. That is something I might say, but to hear you say it . . ." She laughed again, and his mouth dropped open. But she held up her hands. "It's quite alright. I agree. You and I get on very well, don't we?" She smiled. "Though I suspect that most women would feel the same when with you." She put a hand on his arm. "Perhaps we should head back inside?"

He nodded and led her out the doors of the greenhouse and down the path without saying much. Before Lucy and Conor were in earshot, he murmured, "You doubt my sincerity."

She turned to him, feeling bolder than she had in a long time. "No, it's not that."

"It's simply that you have met the deeper Stewart brother, and I sound like air in comparison to his rock."

She sucked in a breath. She'd never thought such a thing, but his words rang true. Still, she didn't want to be calling Lord Featherstone shallow, for he was not. "I would not say something so drastic. You are certainly deep. And, of course, Lord Stewart is also deep." She sighed. "I think it best I retire for the evening before my tired mind says something I don't even mean to say."

"You do not have to be anything clever or witty with me tonight. I understand. And no matter what comes of our talks, I'm certain the Brighton Season will be a grand adventure for us all." He laughed. "Come, let us both give ourselves some rest. Tomorrow I'd like to come by with a phaeton before we must begin preparing for the ball."

"Oh, that sounds lovely."

"I am inclined to take a look at the Strand from a loftier perspective. So many promenading would be an excellent study of people. I wish to get my footing before I throw myself in all the way, if you know what I mean." For a moment, the ever-confident Lord Featherstone appeared somewhat insecure.

Grace was quite charmed by the thought. "I do! That sounds exactly like what I would wish to do as well."

"Perfect. Then I shall be here at an unearthly early hour, but it shall be worth it."

"Thank you."

They walked together back into the house, where she was met by Lord Stewart and Morley. Lucy and Conor entered behind them.

"And how was your walk?" Lord Stewart asked their whole group.

"Enlightening." Lord Featherstone grinned. "And now, I feel we have enjoyed this fine hospitality long enough. Shall we depart and at last leave you lovely people to yourselves?"

The Morleys' carriage pulled to the front of the home.

Lord Featherstone bowed to them all and then alighted into the carriage first.

Lord Stewart stared after his brother's form for a moment then turned to Grace and bowed over her hand. "A pleasure, as always." The lips he pressed to her glove remained a moment longer than was typical. Her hand and arm were rewarded with a rush of sensation she'd never felt before. As her eyes searched his, they seemed as friendly as ever, nothing more amorous than she'd ever seen before in him. But her hand and arms would beg to differ. Something was definitely different than it had ever been where he was concerned.

She nodded and then bid her farewells to the other Mr. Stewarts. But none gave any reaction whatsoever to their touch.

Lucy, Morley, and Grace stood on the porch, waving their farewells until the carriage was out of sight. As soon as they could, Lucy tugged Grace into the house and all three of them rushed up to June's room.

They were quiet, not wishing to wake her, but before they even approached the door, she called, "Oh, come in. I missed everything."

Grace climbed up onto the bed. Lucy joined her, and Morley took the chair at her side.

June reached for Grace's hand. "So, you had the entire Stewart family here in our house today?"

"We did." Lucy nodded. "And they're all highly eligible. Lord Featherstone seems willing and amiable and good."

June turned to Grace. "And what do you think about this?"

"At first I was completely overwhelmed. I did not know what to think of any of it, as in, how I'm supposed to know who to marry. This is precisely why I wanted you to decide. Oh, June. I wish you were able to meet them properly."

"I as well. I shall have to live through your descriptions of them. Come now. Tell me."

"He's kind and careful and works hard. He knows what to say to comfort and ease my burdens."

"Goodness, Lord Featherstone sounds like a wonderful option for you."

Grace frowned. "Oh dear, no. I was talking about Mr. Stewart who is actually *Lord* Stewart—he has a title and we didn't even know that. Morley asked that he stick close and advise me. He is the perfect choice to do so. Ever since he agreed to assist, I have felt greatly at ease."

June turned to Morley for a moment, and they had some

sort of silent conversation. But when she turned her gaze back to Grace, she was all smiles. "I am so happy to hear it. What do you think of Lord Featherstone?"

"He's pleasing enough. Many would find him greatly attractive. That man could be charming anywhere. And he could make hogs sound exciting."

June nodded slowly. "Sounds most excellent as well, I think."

"Oh yes, I have no complaints. And he seems to be most desirous for a match, or at least explore the possibility." Grace lay her head down next to June. "It's been a rather exhausting time. Lord Stewart said the most amazing things in his sermon. I have never been more chastised, while at the same time loved." She sighed, then closed her eyes. The world went quiet. And she fell into a blissful sleep.

Someone shook her shoulder. She opened her eyes but couldn't make sense of what she saw. June, Morley, and Lucy were still all within sight. "Is it morning?"

"No, you are not sleeping until you explain yourself."

"Hmm?" Grace blinked.

"Do you love Lord Stewart?" June's soft voice, her wide eyes, penetrated all the remaining sleep that was threatening, and Grace bolted upright. "No." "But you said . . ." Grace searched her mind, cleared her fuzziness. "I said I'd never felt more loved. It was a spiritual feeling. I just knew I could be better but knew I was still loved anyway. It's a godlike feeling, I think. I don't know. Ask Lord Stewart. He was very good at explaining it in his sermon."

Lucy nodded. "It was indeed a most moving speech, and Grace seemed to be most affected by it."

Grace looked from one to the other. "Is there a problem with that? Did you not enjoy it?"

"I too enjoyed it." Morley nodded. "Nothing wrong at all. I'm pleased as can be that the man is happy to assist you in this search. It's a trying time for us all."

June frowned. "I'm terribly sorry."

Morley stood and kissed her forehead. "June my darling. No, please do not apologize. As we've all said, there is also no rush here. We will see what comes of all this and wait longer if need be."

Grace nodded but wasn't exactly certain what she most wanted. Did she want to marry as soon as possible or wait?

"As the first huge event will be tomorrow, let's have a talk about what kinds of men we would like to join our family." Lucy looked from one to the other, her hands clasped together.

"Good idea. What are your thoughts?" June squeezed Grace's hand.

Lucy sat up straighter. "I think since you have the choice of almost anyone in the world, why not look for a man of title who is wealthy, strong, happy, has a good sort of personality that doesn't argue much with anyone—"

Morley laughed. "Are you looking for someone perfect?"

"Well, yes." Lucy nodded. "And why not? You meet all those expectations. Why could we not find another like you?"

Morley dipped his head in appreciation. "And your Conor is an excellent chap. You two are quite happy."

"Yes, we are." She sighed. "But there aren't many circumstances where you can marry so far below your station and have everything be smoothed over so nicely. You must consider the respectability of a person. If you can, find a man who will provide carriages and servants and a modiste, the things that make it easy for you to move about in Society. Someone who enjoys the dinners and the parties is also most useful. It will assist in the furtherance of your children amongst those of the *ton* when it is their turn to marry."

"Lucy. You're already planning the marriages of my children?"

"Why not? I've planned for mine. It is something to consider."

June lifted her other hand into the air. "Lucy is correct, of course, but first and foremost, consider your happiness. Can you be happy with him? Those things Lucy suggested add to happiness because they limit the worries that some marriages might have. But they aren't the source of happiness."

"You think I should encourage Lord Featherstone?"

"He would be a good match, yes. How is his wealth?" Lucy turned to Morley who tipped his head to the side. "I do believe some of the attraction on his end is for Grace's dowry."

The women gasped.

"But that is not an overly bad thing. Some men are only permitted to marry those with dowries. Their income requires it. Not the man's fault, if you know what I mean."

"True. Men are very practical about these things." Lucy had been fully planning an arranged marriage before she went against all convention and married Conor. "It would be nice to know that you yourself were a part of the attraction though, wouldn't it? Not just your dowry?" Lucy looked from one to the other in their group.

"Certainly, in a love match. Otherwise, it is good to see if you get on well together. Do you picture life the same way?" June closed her eyes. "I know it will work out wonderfully for you, Grace, just like it did for all of us."

Grace loved her sister. What a challenge it must be to lie in bed all day every day, hoping and worrying your child didn't come too early. "Let's leave you to sleep, June. Thank you everyone for your help with this. Before now, I've been concerned about my Season, but I do admit to being excited to wear my first truly formal gown."

June opened her eyes. "Oh, you will be exquisite. That's the loveliest gown I've ever seen. Kate helped design it, you know."

"I know. And afterward, I want a meeting just like this one, where we talk about every man who talks to me."

They all laughed. "Certainly. Too bad we cannot invite Lord Stewart up here in June's room." Morley took his wife's hand and sat closer.

Grace tried to laugh at that as well, but the noise became caught in her throat. Suddenly the image of Lord Stewart, sprawled across the bed, his handsome face laughing with the family, stole her breath.

"I cannot be having those thoughts." She pressed a hand to her chest and when the others stared at her, Lucy's mouth opened, she amended, "I'm kidding. Of course, he's not coming up here, and of course, I'm not thinking of it."

How nice though it would be to have a man in her life, whoever it may be, that would eventually feel comfortable with the other members of her family. She sighed in happiness at the thought. "Let's just get this going, shall we?"

June squeezed her hand again. "We are doing our best, love. Now, off to bed before you fall asleep here again."

The others mumbled agreements and she and Lucy and made their way to their own beds.

As Grace's maid was assisting in preparing her for bed, she thought again about the sermon. One sentence in particular kept coming back to her. *"Think only on the past as it gives you pleasure. What are you becoming now? Who will you be tomorrow?"*

What kind of man could create such a beautiful sentiment? Lord Stewart was remarkable indeed and obviously had very little use for the frivolities of a courtship or even the practice of marriage. At least they could be friends. She lay in bed and pulled the covers up to her chin, hugging herself. And she would have his assistance in finding a man who might be just as good as he.

Was she in love with Lord Stewart? Of course not. They'd hardly related with one another, except to work and serve. But her hunt for marriage was not about love. Her sisters had spoken of men she might attempt to marry. They didn't sound approving of someone in Lord Stewart's meager circumstances.

The largest problem being, he didn't think of her in a marrying way, at least she assumed as much based on their interactions.

She turned over on her side. Everyone was in love with Lord Stewart, or they should be. Now was not the time to be pining for a man who obviously didn't want the same things. She'd be grateful for his assistance and leave things as they should be.

At that thought, she closed the issue in her mind and closed her eyes as well, thinking she'd found the end of things.

But sleep did not come easily.

CHAPTER 12

*C*harles left the house early. He'd somehow acquired a phaeton to use to take Miss Grace out for a ride. He'd dressed in his finest overcoat and taken extra care with his hair. The man acted as though he was determined to win Miss Grace's heart.

Oliver told himself that was grand. But he felt anything but grand.

And he'd not secured a set at the ball with Miss Grace yet. He had every confidence that Charles would secure the first set if he hadn't already, and Miss Grace might run out of sets to give. Oliver was determined that he should dance with her.

Dancing would certainly show her that he was not simply a vicar but a man who could provide her with love.

She'd not spoken of love in her plan to marry. But every woman wanted to be loved—every person did. And with a woman like Miss Grace, he felt himself very capable of such a thing. A marriage of love, not simply convenience, was a rare and beautiful opportunity. All the Standish sisters had acquired such a thing for themselves. Why should Miss Grace be any different? She deserved every happiness.

And so did he.

Every moment with her was adding a rising frustration and impatience in him he'd never known before. And this ball would change things. He was determined to prove to her that she could want him in other ways besides the confidant-friend figure. Or worse, the vicar-religious figure. There just wasn't anything physically desirable in a vicar simply by definition.

Although, what did George say the women were calling him in London? The Handsome Vicar? That had a nice ring. Perhaps if Miss Grace were to hear that others found him handsome...

What he wanted to do was to rush over there and beat Charles to it, to gift her something or share poetry or some other sort of romantic notion before they went on their phaeton ride. He groaned. The problem was, he was going up against the professional wooer of women. No man could win a woman that Lord Featherstone had placed in his sights to win.

With those melancholy thoughts, Oliver joined his brothers in the front sitting room, his notebook and quill in hand.

"And look who is brooding." Jacob pointed. "What did I tell you?"

"What do you mean by brooding? I'm simply coming to sit in the sun with my brothers while I take notes for my next sermon."

They stood. Jacob saluted. "Our que to leave."

"No, stay. Why must you go?"

"We don't wish to interrupt your holy thoughts while you concoct another masterpiece and convince your lady to fall in love with you." Jacob laughed.

George nodded. "He's right, you know. She was swept off her feet by your words."

But Oliver just shook his head. "No, that is the problem precisely. I need her to be thinking of me as something entirely different, a . . . rogue." He placed his pen down on the table top. "That's it. I need to be desirable and dangerous and a bit of a mystery, don't I?"

Jacob and George shared a glance and then they both burst into laughter. George shook his head. "No, that is not it for you. You don't want to be anything but yourself."

"Well, to be truthful, perhaps a more diverting version of yourself might do the trick." Jacob nodded.

"What do you mean more diverting?" Oliver considered his interactions with Miss Grace. "How am I to do that?"

"Is there anything fun to do here in Brighton?"

"Oh, certainly. All the time."

"Well then, see if you and she can both be at the same place, having fun together." Jacob pointed his finger as though he was expressing the most unique and clever idea in the world.

"That's lovely, brother. But so far, I've not seen many opportunities to see her anywhere, let alone a fun location where she and I might enjoy ourselves."

George picked a piece of lint from his pant leg. "The problem here is, the one to talk to is Charles, but he—"

"Yes, I know, the expert is the one who is also trying to

win her over." Oliver gave up trying to write a single thing. "Do you think he cares for her?"

"He's obviously interested." Jacob examined his fingers. "Do you know how many women Charles sees on a regular basis, how many wait in a ballroom, hoping he will ask them?"

"Do I want to know?"

"You probably don't. But I mention his experience because Miss Grace is the first woman he's made some real efforts with." George's shrug was not carefree. He offered a helpful warning.

Oliver pressed his lips together.

The day passed with similar thoughts and repetitive moments where he felt like a brooding, nonsensical bumpkin. His brothers left, his housekeeper avoided him, and he didn't even like his own company until right around the time he started getting ready for the ball. It was then he made a decision, another one, regarding Miss Grace.

Right when his brothers were all back in the house and beginning their own preparations, Oliver stepped out the door.

One of the windows upstairs creaked open and Jacob stuck his head out. "Where are you going?"

"I'm off to the castle. I'll see you chaps at the ball." He mock bowed and then twirled his cane in his hand while he made his way down the familiar path. He'd been asked to be her confidant, her support through this choice. He determined it was time to start using what he could to his advantage.

As soon as he arrived, Morley ushered him in. "I'm so

happy to see you, Lord Stewart. It seems we are already in need of your services."

He didn't even attempt to hide the smile that immediately filled his face. "Do you? How might I be of service?"

"She's all in a dither about what to wear." He shook his head. "And her sister Kate is not here yet. She's designed this dress, but it's a bit forward thinking, as all Kate's designs are. And at the last minute, Grace is worried—"

"Morley, please. Don't tell poor Lord Stewart all about my dresses." Grace peered down over the edge of the balcony. "Besides, we've got it sorted. And hello there, Lord Stewart. I'll be down shortly."

"Hello! I'm pleased to hear it."

"I'm pleased as well." Morley grimaced and turned back to Oliver. "If at all possible, consider avoiding your household while preparing for a ball."

"You see, I'm far from mine."

"Too true. Excellent judgement. Perhaps we shall go for a walk ourselves?" He turned this way and that, as though expecting a summons at any moment.

Oliver laughed. "Are they almost ready, do you think?"

"I have no way of knowing, but if I were to guess, I'd say we have many hours yet."

"Hours?" He pulled out his watch fob. "They wish to arrive reasonably late, then."

"Oh no, they wish to arrive so that Grace does not miss the first set, with which both have agreed-upon dances."

He nodded, feeling unclear about Lord Morley's answers. "I'm unsure how best to assist this evening. Perhaps I shall stay close, be available to counsel, dance with her myself?"

"Excellent, all of those things. The more time you spend with her, the less I need to worry." He grimaced. "I hope you don't feel like I'm neglecting my duties."

"Not at all." Oliver tried to maintain a bland expression. "I will plan to be at her side at all moments, except when she is dancing. Perhaps I'll even ask for two sets." He acted as though nothing were of large importance, but he was almost holding his breath, wondering what Lord Morley would think about his continued presence through the ball.

His grin widened. "Excellent. We will thank you many times over, I imagine."

"It is my pleasure—"

"I'm finally ready." Miss Grace began her descent on the stairs.

Oliver turned, and whatever he was about to say left him completely. She was a vision. Her dress was white and somehow luminous. She almost floated. He'd always thought her an angel and now she looked the part to perfection. Her smile was hesitant but caring. Her face . . . He could not stop looking at her.

Lord Morley said something that Oliver did not hear. Instead, his feet moved him up the stairs and quickly to her side. "Miss Grace." He offered his arm.

"*Lord* Stewart." She placed her hand in the crook of his elbow. "You're looking fine tonight."

"Thank you. A bit different from the Sunday sermon, is it not?"

"It is indeed."

"And you are as beautiful as I've ever seen you. A vision."

Her cheeks colored, and she turned away, her other hand brushing against her skirts as they made their way down the rest of the stairs. "I feel beautiful. Kate is so smart with the dresses she designs. She knew this fabric would be perfect." She paused and put a hand to her lips. "But I'm certain you don't wish to be discussing dress fabrics. You are here enough and so close to the family, I forget that you're a man and that you have interests other than my dresses and what not." She laughed. "And I'm talking without stop. Please say something so that I may hush."

He placed a hand over the top of hers. "No, I love to hear what's in your mind. Be it a fleeting thought of minor importance or your deepest, most heartfelt desires. I wish to know them all. Speak freely, and I will be the happiest in your company."

"Then I shall, but you first." She nudged him. "How was your day? I missed you when only Lord Featherstone came in the phaeton."

"Did you?" He couldn't help the pleased smile that grew on his face. "I should have come, even just to see you off. I was instead brooding in my lonely state in my front room."

"Brooding?" She shook her head. "I cannot imagine such a thing in you."

"I shall not describe myself, for no one needs to imagine such things. But you shall have to believe me. I discovered anew that I am unhappy when not at your side. It's as simple as that." They paused on the stairs. They had but four to go, but Miss Grace studied him and he would not break her gaze for anything in the world. Their eyes connected in a new way, it seemed, as he watched thoughts cross her face.

"You are more spectacular than you realize, Miss Grace."

Something broke the spell and she looked away. "Thank

you, I feel quite ordinary, I assure you, and if you carry on so, I shall become quite captured by my own importance. We can't have that. I assure you there is plenty you do not know about me that might convince you of my many failings . . ."

Lord Morley chuckled. "Grace? Failings? Do not believe such a thing."

They turned to him, having arrived at the bottom of the stairs.

"We shall ride in the first carriage. I do not know when the others will be ready, but we are, so let us be off! Who has your first set, Grace?"

She sucked in a breath. "Oh! Yes. Lord Featherstone has claimed it."

"Do you have others still available?" Oliver led her out into the main entryway, following Lord Morley.

"I do. There are several."

"Might I come claim you for one, then? I hear that the prince enjoys the waltz. Might I have that set?"

"Do you waltz?" She studied him anew again, and he hoped she saw more each time.

"I do, in fact. I had quite a full life before coming here as vicar; however, I'd not dance it with just anyone." He held her gaze again.

"Then, certainly. I'd love to dance the waltz with you. I'm not as practiced."

"Not to worry. I shall welcome all nudges from your slippers and cover any missteps, though I imagine you are far more adept than I." He led her out the door and handed her up into the carriage.

Lord Morley tapped his shoulder before Oliver followed her in. "You're just the man for the job. Thank you again."

He nodded. "Happy to be of service." He wasn't certain how to respond. Surely Lord Morley could see that more than mere friendliness or duty was playing a part here.

But the look on Grace's face when he arrived at her side in the carriage said she'd heard their conversation. "So, what exactly is your role here with me tonight? Are you to be helping me choose suitors?" She looked away.

"I . . ." He cleared his throat, unsure how to continue. "We talked of my being a support to you . . ."

With Lord Morley joining them, he did not feel free to be more bold in his declarations. But before the night was out, he planned to tell her exactly how he intended to move forward, where she was concerned.

She adjusted her skirts. "I assure you that I don't need a nursemaid at the ball."

"I wasn't suggesting or hoping to play that role, believe me." He reached for her hand. "You are important to me. You were concerned, so I'm here to aid in any way you desire." He cleared his throat again. "And I would also like the pleasure of dancing with you, perhaps the dinner set as well if it is available."

She frowned. "You are hoping to dance two sets with me? As well as assisting in finding my husband?" She shook her head. "What exactly is this?"

"I . . ." He glanced at Lord Morley for assistance.

Lord Morley seemed curious for his answer but he jumped in. "Oh, Grace, be nice. He's offered to help us out. You can't blame the man for wanting a bit of diversion while he's at it, can you?"

Her gaze softened somewhat. "And you think dancing with me will bring enjoyment?"

"It's the only reason I asked. I haven't asked another for any set at this ball."

"You haven't?" Her eyes widened again, and to his great relief, they had returned somewhat to their previous closeness.

Until Lord Morley laughed. "He'll likely not have time for any other sets at any rate. He's agreed to not leave your side the whole of the ball."

She gasped and leaned away from him. "What? No. Lord Stewart, you are not obligated to stand at my side the whole of the ball."

"It's not an obligation, believe me. I will welcome the chance."

A great look of discomfort crossed her face.

"Unless you'd rather I not . . ."

"It's not that I don't enjoy your company. And our sets will be lovely. Please come fetch me also for the dinner set. But no. I can't have our vicar standing at my side throughout Prinny's ball." She colored a bit as she said the words, but her expression was sincere.

She found him socially embarrassing?

"I see." Oliver nodded. "Then perhaps I will be there if you need to consult. But otherwise, you wish me to be invisible?" He couldn't help himself. The hurt he felt as her true impression of him came pouring out of her mouth was now coming out in his own words.

"Invisible . . . no." She looked away. "This is terribly untoward. I apologize." She looked to Lord Morley who didn't say anything, a pained look resting on his face. "Surely you understand. It is my very first ball." She turned pleading eyes to Oliver for some sort of affirmation of her rejection of his calling and position.

He tried to pretend to understand. He knew what his brothers would say. They would agree with her. But after spending so much time caring for others, working in his employment, it had become much more than simply a manner in which to earn his keep. He could not make things easier for her. "I see nothing in my profession that would be limiting to your social standing. But in some crowds, particularly Prince George's close friends, perhaps a pious preacher is not the man to turn to for diversion." He tried not to strain against his cravat. His brothers had been correct. He was not seen as fun.

"Oh dear. I've hurt your feelings." Her wide, sad eyes were his undoing.

He shook his head. "No, not at all. I am pleased to be assisting in this manner. I have the utmost respect and gratitude for your family and for all you do to support the vicarage. I am at your service, Miss Grace, in whatever ways would be most useful."

She nodded, her expression clearing somewhat. But the previous closeness, his flirting, and the moments where he felt like he was more to her than simply a religious counselor seemed to have slipped away.

Time to drastically change her impression of him. Or give up. And he was not one to quit.

CHAPTER 13

*G*race wished she could erase the hollow expression on Lord Stewart's face from her memory. And now, she'd do just about anything to soften the blank, emotionless one.

They arrived at the ball together. She walked in on his arm. But he said precious little, and when he did, it was in highly proper tones.

They both met Prince George together. He had much to say to Morley and then polite things to say to Lord Stewart. When the prince turned to her, he smiled. "Now here is a bit of fresh air in my ballroom. Please enjoy yourself, and if you have a set, I'd love to dance." He bowed over her hand with a charming expression.

For a moment, she was completely breathless and in shock. Lord Stewart pulled her hand close to his side in a gentle nudge.

"Oh yes, thank you for the honor. My third set is free."

"Third it is." He smiled again, his eyes lingering as she moved on.

"Did that just happen?" She sucked in her breath, leaning closer to Lord Stewart in a loud whisper.

"Yes, and perhaps you should stand up a little straighter and act like the noble you are."

His tone was not exactly harsh but definitely not chummy. A moment of irritation surged inside her, and she did stand taller and considerably farther away from him. "Yes, thank you."

"Very good. Now, remember who you are, Miss Grace, and act in that knowledge. The ballroom is at your feet." He gestured with his hand to a room full of people.

The master of ceremonies took a card with their names. "Lord Morley, Miss Grace Standish, Lord Stewart."

With the announcement of his name, more than a few female eyes turned in their direction. For the first time, Grace considered her friendly vicar through the eyes of the ladies of the *ton*.

And she was astounded.

Women approached. He had not yet noticed or seen or acknowledged them, but they were coming. And all had a look, a certain interest, that Grace could not deny. She wished to tug him closer again.

But then Morley closed the gap between them. "If I might steal Miss Grace for a moment, some introductions to start us off would be highly useful."

"Excellent." Lord Stewart nodded, a perceptible but small motion of his head, and then he turned toward the crowd of women who were nearly upon him.

So he had seen them.

The closest clung to his arm immediately, fanning herself and laughing with bright smiles. And she introduced three others. All of which were equally pleased.

"What is happening to Lord Stewart?"

Morley laughed. "Did you not know? They are calling him the Handsome Vicar or something. He's all the talk right now. Ask Kate about it when she comes. I think she even did a drawing of him."

Grace could not take her eyes away from Lord Stewart. He was laughing and charming in a whole new way. The women blushed and flustered and primped around him like a bunch of unfurling peacocks, and all at once, Grace wanted nothing more to do with it.

"Who are these introductions?" She turned back to Morley.

"Oh, just these matrons over here. And their sons. But truly, I hoped to free up our good vicar for them." He pointed with his chin, drawing her attention back to the women.

"You did what? Morley, really."

"What? He's a man. He's in need of a wife. I thought to do the chap a favor. He's done so much for us. And you are feeling touchy about his agreement to stand by you instead of feeling grateful. He's a good man, Grace."

"I know he's a good man. I've heard his sermons."

"But Grace, he's a man." He indicated the women again, and she refused to look. "With all that available attention, he has two sets with you and has offered to spend the whole of the ball at your side." He stared at her long enough that her mind spun with several different possibilities for his actions.

"Do you . . . what are you saying?"

"I'm not saying anything. I cannot see into the man's mind or his motivations. But he deserves our gratitude much more than our disdain."

"Perhaps I would have benefitted, even socially, with such a man at my side."

"You would have, and our social standing is not the most important way to benefit. Remember that as you try to navigate all of this." He waved another hand, indicating a filling room.

"I owe him an apology."

"One he is likely to accept, but will he ever think the same way about your friendship? Perhaps you have more to show than simply a repentant heart."

She couldn't even begin to puzzle through what Morley was trying to say. "I'll figure out Lord Stewart. In the meantime, let's get these introductions out of the way before the first set."

"Ah yes, you also have Lord Featherstone to contend with."

"Contend?"

"He's a brilliant man, handsome, talented, charming."

"But?"

"No buts. He's at the top of my list at the moment."

She nodded, unsure what exactly Morley was trying to say. They had approached a remarkably overdressed woman. She sat in a chair, almost lost underneath all her finery. Many folds of fabric and deep reds and golds billowed up all around her. Something in her eyes sparkled in familiarity. "Your Grace?"

Morley laughed and bowed. "The Duchess of York. Do you remember our Miss Grace?"

"Of course I do," the older woman snapped, but her mouth filled with smile. "Come sit by me, dear. We have much to discuss."

"Oh yes, mum." She sat immediately at the older woman's side. "It is good to see you again." She was so much altered in appearance but much the same in temperament it seemed.

"Yes, I imagine it is. Now, we don't have a lot of time. I hear you're seeking an arrangement."

"I am." She swallowed back her rising irritation. Could Morley not keep the whole matter to himself?

"Oh, don't fuss at Lord Morley. He's in need of assistance. And he talked to the right woman. This ballroom is full of men. All of which would be happy to have a chance with you."

"All?"

"Yes, all. They're not stupid, though they act it sometimes. They could each use more blunt in their coffers, pardon my rather rude manner. I just want to be perfectly plain. But you need to see which ones are the sincere ones and which ones are playing nice for a time."

"That's exactly why I asked Lord Morley to arrange things for me, and June too, but she's stuck at home."

"I heard, yes. Unfortunate timing of her confinement. I'll be paying a visit this week. But you're not thinking clearly about this. Lord Morley will never be able to judge the sincerity of a man's affections."

"He won't?"

"Certainly not. Only you can see that."

Grace sunk lower in her chair. "But I cannot." The world started to darken around her. "I asked for help because I'm a terrible judge of who is a good man and who not."

"Nonsense. You are older now. You see things clearly. Look around. Can you not tell just by watching conversations who is making fun and who means what they say?"

Grace's brief cursory glance told her nothing of the kind.

"Trust your instincts, my dear."

"Hmm." Her stomach clenched in all kinds of new agony. She would never be able to know.

The instruments began tuning.

"Ah, you'll be looking for your first dance partner, or he'll be looking for you. Let me see if I can guess the one." Her sharp gaze flitted around the room.

Grace could not see Lord Featherstone yet. "I don't think . . ."

A commotion began at the far side of the room. People's chatter rose in greater volume, and all at once, the crowds parted. Lord Featherstone walked toward her, women dropping away as he went, and all eyes on him did not make his approach anything less than shattering to Grace's nerves.

"Ho ho! Lord Featherstone, is it?" She clucked. "Hmm."

"What is it, Mum?" Grace turned to her.

But all she could do is laugh. "You'll enjoy this one, my dear. I'm certain of it."

Grace stood.

Lord Featherstone bowed before her. "Miss Grace. I saw you the moment I walked in." He then turned to the Duchess of York. "Your Grace, do you mind terribly if I steal away the brightest light in the room?"

"Not one bit, my lord. You two enjoy yourselves."

"I will count this as the highlight of the whole night,

believe me." Lord Featherstone nodded to the venerable woman and then led Grace out onto the floor.

"Are you well-known here, in Brighton?" She looked all around them, and people were attentively watching.

"Most of this crowd comes from London. They arrived at the announcement of a ball at the Royal Pavilion. And I do live in London. Many of them are my acquaintances, yes."

A couple came to stand beside them. The man winked at Lord Featherstone. "We've never been happier. We're expecting now, though I'm not allowed to say, except to you."

"John, hush." The woman colored a pretty pink.

Grace turned to her. "Congratulations."

"Oh, thank you. John isn't supposed to tell, but since we owe all our happiness to Lord Featherstone, I guess I can forgive this one time." She smiled, her face full of love.

And then the music began.

As Grace approached Lord Featherstone, she tilted her head. "They owe all their happiness to you?"

"Oh, well, you know. I introduced them. That sort of thing."

She nodded. "Hmm."

They circled each other, then he took her hands. "How was your afternoon?"

"Lovely. I tried on a few dresses." She laughed. "And Lord Stewart helped me settle on this one." Or at least, his reaction reassured her she'd made the right choice.

Lord Featherstone's eyebrows rose. "Did he?" He looked down their line of dancers.

Lord Stewart had joined them with a brilliantly

gorgeous blonde-haired woman. "He does have excellent taste."

"Does he?"

"Oh yes, before he became a vicar, he was the paragon of fashion in our circles."

She nearly choked. "Wh—"

"But don't ever let on that I told you. He'd never dress that way now. It would not be seemly for his profession." He flicked his fingers. "Or some such thing. He says similar things about loud diversions and even attending balls. He needs someone to remind him he is a man, as well as a vicar." He tilted his head in the direction of his brother's dancing form. "This right here. This will remind him."

"I see." She lifted her hands while she spun again in the opposite direction. "I hear people are calling him the Handsome Vicar."

"Oh yes. Well, when he left London, it was with a great amount of dissatisfaction, you see. He seems to think the whole lot of us are too frivolous, too uncaring, and dare I suggest, insincere." He tsked. "He left rather abruptly and, in his wake, a great hole remained. Which has yet to be filled." He shrugged. "They miss him."

Lord Featherstone's other brothers had also joined the line to dance.

"You are quite the spectacle, you four."

"We tend to be, yes, but that is neither here nor there. I must compliment you on your dress. It glows almost as brightly as your complexion."

"Thank you. It was my sister Kate's idea. She has quite a talent for these things."

"She does indeed and writes for the *Whims and Fancies*, I

hear." His one brow quirked up. "Did a number on me the other month."

Grace laughed. "She's been known to do that. I apologize if it brought you any unwanted attention."

"Never fear. It was all very much wanted."

Grace pressed her lips together as she turned away, meeting Morley's watchful gaze. He raised his brows in question, but she turned back around, facing Lord Featherstone again. "Do you seek attention, then?"

"I? For myself? No." He laughed.

When many people turned to them to watch his laugh, he added, "I don't mind it, for example, this is rather fun, all these people watching us, wondering if we are about to make an announcement." He laughed again.

She gasped. "Are they?" She looked all around her at the inquisitive stares.

"Are they what? Watching us? Certainly." He stepped closer than was necessary and toyed with her hair for a fraction of a second.

Half their audience wore triumphant expressions.

"They have their opinions about us, you see."

She shook her head. "And you enjoy this?"

He thought for a moment. "I don't mind it. It's all in fun, after all."

They changed partners. Everyone shifted to the next person and then they all repeated previous steps. She stood across from a handsome gentleman. He was tall, had soft eyes, and gentle hands. "Lord Anston, at your service." He nodded as they circled.

"I'm Miss Grace. Pleased to make your acquaintance."

"Yes, I as well. A famed Standish sister, are you not?"

"Famed? I . . ."

"Certainly. A well-respected sort of fame."

"Ah, well then, thank you."

"Of course." His smile filled his face.

They finished their steps and she moved down the line to two more until she was dancing with the man right before she would then dance with Lord Stewart. Although he had not once looked in her direction, she could not stop glancing his way. Her whole body hummed in expectation to once again be facing him.

CHAPTER 14

Oliver schooled his features. Miss Grace stepped in front of him. He looked down into her hesitant and smiling face, slightly flushed from the dance, glowing from the beauty that was just naturally in her and emanated from her goodness. He smiled back. But it was his old smile from his days in London, during the time when he was attempting to win them all and marry none. He took her hands in his, those good, hardworking, service-minded hands, and they circled.

"How are you liking the ball?" Her voice was friendly.

He nodded. "It's as I expected. Prinny's parties are always a crush."

"Do you see many from Sunday here?"

He faltered for a moment but then shrugged. "I don't think so, but then again, they won't be wanting their vicar at the ball, will they?" He raised an eyebrow.

"Lord Stewart, I'm sorry. I wasn't thinking. Of course, you have a life outside of the vicarage. Of course, you would naturally fit in well at the ball. Of course you would be much sought after. I don't know what I was thinking, to be honest. I wonder if perhaps—"

It was time for them to circle.

When she returned, he widened his eyes, waiting for her to finish the sentence. In truth, he didn't know what she would say.

"I wonder if perhaps I was thinking of how I don't wish to be a burden to you."

Of course, she would be concerned for such things. But certainly, she'd also been concerned for other reasons. "I understand."

"You do?"

"Yes, I do. You did not wish to be socially burdened by a sorry chap with no real skills in that area. You thought that I would perhaps scare away your suitors and friends." He shouldn't have done it. Her face clouded with hurt. But he had to see if she was as shallow as her comment had suggested. Did she care so much about appearing a certain way?

But she crumpled in front of him. "I am afraid I have a little of that in me, yes. And I'm sorry. I really am." She didn't look him in the face after that. They finished the dance with a sad and simpering Miss Grace and then she moved on to the next person.

He felt his brother's eyes on him, and he didn't want to look but he did and saw just what he expected. Strong disapproval. But what had he done, really? Simply expressed her truest feelings back to her face?

Perhaps he shouldn't have done so at the ball.

She continued down the line with partner after partner

and he wanted to bless the man who finally brought a smile back to her face. It was his other brother, George.

He took to the side of the dance floor after that. Some women came to talk or to make introductions, but he kept to himself as much as he could. As he watched Miss Grace dance with partner after partner, he knew he'd made a mistake. She was equally genuine and kind to whoever approached her. She was obviously very sought after.

She had no regard for a person's looks or status that governed the manner in which she treated them. She was a diamond of the first water, certainly, for reasons totally unrelated to her lovely gown, beautiful face, or healthy dowry and connections. She was Miss Grace, and the very woman he'd first been impressed with shined for all to see.

Very few would appreciate that side of her.

He certainly hadn't, not enough.

Charles joined him. "Become a wallflower now, have you?"

"Yes."

"Oh, come off it, man. There are women here who need to dance. Do your duty."

"I am. I'm keeping an eye on Miss Grace."

"Brooding."

"And brooding, I'll admit it. Though I never would have thought myself capable."

Charles straightened his sleeves. "I might marry her."

"You should. If she'll have you."

"Do you mean that?"

Oliver turned to him. "Are you serious about her?"

"She's an excellent catch. She'd make a marvelous wife,

and she would help me in my business. Do you see how good she is with everyone?"

Oliver sighed. "I do. Does she know about your business?"

"No, unless someone has told her."

"Are you going to tell her?"

"I should. I will." He nodded. "Before we sign any papers." He laughed. "But until then, it is simply a pleasure to try to win her heart."

Oliver grunted.

"She speaks mostly of you."

Oliver opened his mouth, mostly surprised and unduly pleased.

"And asks after you."

The tiniest bit of hope lit. "Does she?"

"Oh, stop with your wide puppy eyes. I care nothing for your worthless attempts to brood. This does not win anyone's heart, doesn't endear anyone, and certainly doesn't move forward your goals and aims. If I'm to win a woman out from under my brother, I want it to be a fair fight." He faced him and pressed a finger into his chest. "Do not give up this fight." The fierceness of his expression surprised Oliver, and the pressure into his chest pinged him with a touch of pain.

Charles was gone before Oliver could respond or react.

"How do I overcome my own failings? I'm my worst enemy in this." He mumbled to himself.

"By apologizing." The duchess's voice made him jump.

"Your Grace?"

"Yes, I've been sitting here the entire time."

"I beg your pardon. How do you do?" He bowed.

"Oh, don't bother will all that. Go apologize to the woman. She's worth the effort, as you seem to have noticed."

"Yes, she is." He watched as she finished the latest set with a deep curtsey and an open smile.

"Well." The Duchess tugged on his shirtsleeve. "Go on."

The music to a waltz began. He brushed his shoulders and rotated his neck. "That's my cue."

"That's what I like to see." Her chuckle entertained him as he walked toward Miss Grace. He did most definitely owe her an apology.

As he approached, others also did, obviously asking for her hand, which she graciously turned down, one after another. She glanced up, watching him approach while turning down yet another.

When the measures were concluding their introduction, he bowed before her. "Please forgive my prideful, ungrateful self and accept my hand?"

Her eyes widened.

Realizing what he said, he straightened, taking back his offered hand. "For the dance. Please waltz with me." He shook his head, marveling at how easily the words had slipped out of his mouth. He reached for her again with an embarrassed laugh.

She stepped closer, resting her other hand on his shoulder. "I've been saving you the waltz."

"Thank you for remembering."

"I considered dancing with another. I wasn't certain you still wanted to spend the time with me." She avoided looking him in the eyes.

"Grace." He relished in the intimacy of her name on his

lips. He wished to say it again. But it had the intended effect. She lifted her lashes and the glory of her full blue eyes looked into his yet again. "Forgive me. I was hurt, yes, but I should have accepted your apology, should have assumed you had the best intentions in the first place. I should never have behaved as I have."

They moved about the floor without even thinking about their feet. He watched her, waited, hoped.

When she did not respond at first, his lips tugged up in a smile. "While you're thinking, shall we show off a little bit?"

"What do you mean?" Her eyes flashed with a touch of daring, and as he suspected, she was open to something a little out of the ordinary.

"Just follow my lead." He winked and then he picked up their pace, he lengthened their stride. He started slowly to see if she would follow, and when she did perfectly, he added more flourish.

Soon they were skipping and turning and twirling and spinning and double-timing and then slowing the time by half—whatever their hearts wished as they skimmed the ballroom.

Grace laughed openly and then clung to him with a look of concentration in order to keep step. She moved and swayed and leaned and even dipped with abandon all throughout their waltz until she was quite breathless.

He slowed their pace, as slow as they could and held her closer than ever. "You, Miss Grace, are a lovely dancer." His eyes caressed her face. With every breath, he wished to drink her in. Her lips were slightly parted, full and inviting. He stood as close as he dared but kept himself appropriate.

She deserved the best, most respectful courtship a man could offer. "I . . ."

Lord Featherstone approached them with his partner. "That was some good dancing, brother. I see you learned from our lessons."

He growled deep in his throat and Grace looked up in surprise. "Did he teach you to dance?"

Oliver shook his head. "He did not."

Charles just tipped his head back and laughed while guiding his partner farther away.

"You two are so different, yet so alike." Miss Grace studied him. "And I think I shall forgive you." She bit her lip, a tantalizing pressure right in the center. "If you'll forgive me. It is difficult for me to reconcile the man at the pulpit who speaks with power and makes me feel things I've never felt—godly things—with the man here on the dance floor . . . who also makes me feel things I've never felt. Though perhaps not as godly." She looked down, her cheeks coloring.

Oh, how he wished to kiss away her embarrassment. He had so many things to tell her, so much he'd also like to teach, but he was not at a pulpit. He was dancing with a beautiful woman who'd just admitted her attraction.

"Grace." His whisper filled the air around them. "Look at me."

When she did, he shook his head. "These feelings are godly too." He lifted his hand to cup her face, then ran a thumb along her lower lip.

She leaned into him. The air between them warmed. He stepped as closely as he dared. Her hand ran along the back of his jacket and then her fingers touched the skin on his neck and went up into his hair.

Every sense in him filled with need to close the space between them, to pull her tight, to press his lips to hers. These and a thousand other ways to show her just how much he cared flew through his mind at a rapid pace. But all he did was bring her other hand to his lips. "This has been and will be my most cherished memory from this ball."

She watched his mouth press into her knuckles again and nodded. "The supper set?"

"And the supper set." He held her hand out to the side again. "I believe we have just a few more measures. How about a dramatic dip . . . or?"

She shook her head and stepped close enough to rest her face on his chest. "Let's just stay right here."

He moved them as far into the shadows as he could and swayed with her through the last few measures of their waltz.

Her heart pounded against his.

He held her, wishing to communicate just how precious and important she was to him, then the music ended.

The musicians were taking a break and would return for the last half of the evening, which included their supper.

He was loath to part with her, but he stepped back and then bowed. "Thank you, Miss Grace."

"My pleasure." She dipped into a low and respectful curtsey.

He walked with her back to Lord Morley who stood with two other men. They seemed to be waiting for Miss Grace.

"Do you know them?" Oliver turned to her with a gentle smile.

"No, I don't." Her brow furrowed the slightest bit.

"Well, you'll do famously, whatever this is. Perhaps just two more introductions." But even as he said the words, he suspected that perhaps they were the next two men who Lord Morley had been thinking about for Miss Grace's arrangement. He wanted to pause in their approach and ask Miss Grace quickly if she would like him to talk to Morley . . . and if she wished for him to be considered in an arrangement. But now was not the moment. And he didn't think he himself wished for such a thing. He'd rather be chosen. He wanted to propose and be told yes. If she didn't know enough to accept his hand, then he needed to get to know her better.

While he mused and argued with himself, they came upon the three without him saying another word.

Morley nodded. "Lord Stewart, Miss Grace. I'd like for you to meet two friends visiting from London. This is Lord Haversham and Mr. Templeton."

Miss Grace curtseyed with perfect grace and a polite smile. They each bowed over her hand, and Oliver immediately disliked the boredom in one and the greed in the other. No, neither was good enough for Miss Grace; surely Morley could see that, especially when Charles was in consideration. He was leaps and bounds ahead of either one.

Oliver sounded ridiculous, even to his own ears. He, Oliver, was also to be considered, or at least he hoped he would be. Surely Miss Grace would speak for him.

One of the men asked her to dance and it was a beautiful sight to see her say no, just as Prince George approached. "I believe we have this set?"

He nodded to the two newcomers, then greeted Lord

Morley and Oliver with a smile. "Thank you for sparing her this set. I've been looking forward to it all evening."

Lord Morley bowed. "You're welcome, Your Highness."

He led a smiling Grace out onto the dance floor, and Oliver and Morley both moved closer to the edge of the floor to keep an eye on their prince.

"You never know," Oliver mumbled.

"You are so correct. You never do." They both took on the same stern expression.

"Well then, I think we shall take to cards." Mr. Templeton nodded to Lord Haversham, and they both went in the other direction.

Oliver turned to Morley. "What do they offer this arrangement?"

He shook his head. "I'm not seeing the same things I'd hoped for when corresponding with them. They are eons behind most of the men we know, particularly you Stewart men. I don't know what I was thinking, and worse, now I don't know what to do with them." He sighed, then clapped Oliver on the back. "Perhaps you could assist in that as well? Would you be willing to do a bit of entertaining for us? Take them hunting, fishing, play cards?" He cleared his throat. "Do you participate in games of chance?"

"On occasion, though I don't usually have extra cash to be spending on the cards tables."

"Ah, I understand. While we are on the subject, I've been meaning to ask, do you hope to marry?"

Oliver nodded and swallowed, trying to organize his thoughts that had suddenly taken to flight all over his brain. "I do indeed hope to marry. It's funny you should ask that right now."

"I'm glad to hear it. And you should. A wife for your vicarage would do so much good. It will take a special kind of woman, someone who wishes to go without some of the finer things, someone who doesn't shirk a little work and a lot of hours alone. Perhaps your children will need to marry especially well when considering their finances. It's an interesting situation you're in and a noble one. You've made a sacrifice of sorts, haven't you?"

"I suppose I have." Oliver didn't want to tell him that his ancestral estate was in such bad sorts, he was living better off now than he normally would have been at home with Charles.

Morley crossed his arms, sending a stern expression in Prince George's direction. "I remember the sisters when I first met them. They were cold in their house. They had only the clothes that a few of the magnanimous members of the *ton* would give them, and they counted pennies in order to eat. Grace used to sit by the fire in the kitchen, the only one they could afford to keep up and running and tell June how very much she wanted to always have everything she needed. She would say, 'June, when I marry, I'll never be cold again. Not only will every room be full of heat, but I shall have carriages with warming blocks. Multiple carriages.'"

Oliver smiled, but he couldn't feel the energy of it.

"It became somewhat of a joke between them—that Grace would have to marry a man who could promise enough coal." Morley smiled at him, but there was a hint of something serious in his eyes.

Oliver nodded. "That is quite an endearing story. It is

hard to believe such a lovely family could have come upon such difficult times."

"I've thought of it over and over. Gerald and I are pleased to have been able to bring back some of what they had lost. They are so deserving. Every last one of them."

Oliver agreed wholeheartedly, and his mind went into a great turmoil once again regarding the lovely Miss Grace. Did Morley disapprove of a simple vicar?

Should Oliver step away so that Grace could have the kind of life she deserved? Charles had no money, but he was the Marquis, with an estate that would grow and respond to the influx of her dowry.

New problems plagued him and once again disrupted the rather lovely feelings the two of them had shared in their Waltz.

CHAPTER 15

*W*hile some things had become perfectly clear, Grace was now more confused than ever about some others.

And none of it would be sorted while she danced with Prince George, she was certain of that.

"I noticed you in the corner with our holy vicar." Prince George laughed and winked at her. "Or is he not as holy as I thought? Perhaps I'll come to one of his sermons after all." His laugh filled her ears, and his words were no doubt captured by everyone around them. She wished to die a hundred deaths, while all the others undoubtedly wondered at just what the prince meant.

"He's been a wonderful friend and counselor as I navigate my first Season."

"Oh?" The Prince's mouth twitched. "Has he been giving you advice about who to marry?"

"No, not really." All her inner alarms were going off, and

she knew she should not tell the prince anything she didn't want known. "But he is a good friend."

"Yes, very friendly." He laughed again and then shook his head. "I apologize. I can see that my humor is not appreciated. I do enjoy a good story, so I wondered about the two of you. Do keep me informed if you would. In the meantime, let us enjoy our dance." They moved to the steps of a country dance and soon moved to the other two in their foursome and then back. Everyone around her seemed completely enamored with the prince, but she could only feel shame. Were her actions that noticeable and inappropriate? She thought on the last few measures of their waltz and wished to hang her head. Morley and June might do as much at home, but they were married and mostly alone.

She finished their dance with a smile, but inwardly, she was looking for a reason to escape the ball and return to her room at home.

But alas, she was trapped by agreed-upon dances, by a dinner set with Lord Stewart, and by the insistence of Morley that she stay the course. She inwardly groaned and moaned and sighed and slumped, but outwardly, she smiled and gracefully continued another set with a man she hardly knew.

Throughout it all, Lord Stewart was always within sight; he was attentive. She was comforted by him and his presence, and the longer she thought about things, the more she felt compelled to have a conversation with him. He was the vicar. If their actions were that outside of appropriate behavior, wouldn't he have resisted? But she had no opportunity to talk to him at all until their dinner set. As soon as the music began, she made her way to him as quickly as she could, and her words tumbled out of her as well. "Might we speak? Perhaps a walk on the veranda or in the gardens?"

Lord Stewart looked to his right and left before speaking in a more subdued voice. "Certainly. Is something amiss?"

She shook her head and then shrugged. "I'm unsure. But I'd like your thoughts on the matter."

"Then let us find a quick corner, shall we?"

A woman close enough to listen placed a hand over her mouth and giggled.

Grace turned to her. "No, it's not like that."

"Oh, don't worry about me." She waved at them and hurried away.

"And she will be talking to her friends." Lord Stewart frowned. "Perhaps we should merely stand here in front of all but speak quietly or in our own way of understanding."

"Our own way of understanding?"

"Certainly, like in code. My brothers and I do this at times. For example, I could say, 'You're feeling like you did after meeting the Williamses for the first time.'"

She had been miserable when meeting the Williamses. "I see. Yes. I am feeling like that, but a milder version."

His eyes filled with concern. "We must find a remedy."

"I danced with the largest person in the room."

Understanding lit his eyes. "And also the most vulgar, if I might be blunt."

She nodded. "I can well see that."

He stiffened and moved her more into the shadows. "How well can you see that?"

"Oh, not that well." She nodded. "Apologies, I am not practiced at speaking in code. But he did notice the final measures of my favorite dance."

His eyes lit with pleasure. "Your favorite dance?"

She smiled, her face heating. "Oh stop. Yes. But the problem at hand... he had questions and suppositions."

He lifted his head and searched the room. "Ah."

"I wondered if there was anything to be worried about. I mean, you are the vicar here. I would hope you would know these things."

"That was not very code."

"Well?"

"So before I became this vicar of which you speak, I was more open with my affections." His face was full of apology. "Very careful about those things, but yes, more open. And more giving of my attention." He cleared his throat, his own face turning a slight pink. "I was careful during my favorite dance to, ahem, shield us from most prying eyes."

She shook her head. "So you're saying you're an expert at being a rake?"

He coughed. "I am not saying that. Here, my dear, is where codes are not precise and can lead to misunderstanding. I have never been or will ever be a rake." He stared into her face with such a look of complete sincerity that she chose to believe him.

"Then what are you saying?"

"I'm simply saying that very few noticed us. I made certain and I was careful." He lifted his eyebrows. "But it was a moment I would not change, and it was so . . . important to me that I couldn't resist lingering for just a few measures."

Her mouth dropped and then she nodded. "But the prince?"

"Is a regular cad."

She gasped. "You mustn't say such things." It was her turn to look around them.

People were starting to notice.

He held out his arm. "Now I think it is time for us to take our set. I do believe this one is mine?"

"Yes, it is." She shook her head, mildly pleased and somewhat shocked at his admissions. "I thought I knew you, Lord Stewart."

"You do."

She would like to believe such a thing. "There are many different sides to you, I am seeing."

"Perhaps. But of all those, you have seen who I am more than anyone." His confidence poured from him. He was suddenly a handsome desirable man, as well as a respected and worthy man of faith.

"I hope that is true." They faced each other. "The Mr. Stewart I know is a man I would greatly care to know and learn from."

"And Lord Stewart?"

She felt her face heat again. "He has certainly grabbed my attention."

He stood taller. A wildly triumphant look enveloped his face, so much so that she laughed. "Then I have accomplished my designs."

"Which are?"

"To show you that underneath this vicar is a man with feelings and energy and needs. I'm a man." He leaned closer while they came together to circle one another. "Who has an abiding interest in you."

They separated again, and she felt the need to fan herself or get a drink or something. Never had she imagined that the wonderful, kind, and attentive vicar could house such a bold and enticing interior. She found herself wildly enamored. But from her past experience, those were dangerous and distracting emotions, and they almost certainly clouded her judgment.

Judgment she happily allowed to be clouded though as she faced him in the dance and sat with him at dinner and laughed with him on the veranda.

Lord Stewart stood close, his hand reaching out to toy with one of her curls. "These fascinate me. How can hair do such a thing?"

She laughed and stepped nearer. He was just so enjoyable, until Lord Featherstone came to fetch her for his set, the final one of the evening.

"There you are. I'm happy you are out here safe with the vicar instead of in the hands of a more undesirable seduction." His gaze moved from one to the other, half teasing, half serious.

Grace gasped.

"Apologies to your sensitive ears." He grinned and held out his arm and winked at Lord Stewart. "Thank you for taking such excellent care of my partner." He placed a protective hand over hers and with a wink, led them out toward the dance floor.

The music to a waltz began, this time a foursome.

Grace could have laughed out loud if Lord Stewart had been near enough to hear her.

"You find this amusing."

"I do."

"Let me guess. You are most amused that you will have danced both waltzes this evening with a Stewart."

"I am." She nodded in his direction. "How astute of you."

"You will find that more than anything, I am a great noticer of persons."

"I think you said that once already." They moved in the three steps of the waltz and she found her confidence had grown. Time with Lord Stewart had helped her see things from a bolder perspective.

His eyes twinkled at her. "I did, in fact. I wanted to make sure you remembered."

Her mouth wiggled in a half smile. "I don't think I'm likely to forget."

"Excellent."

"I'm a noticer of things as well."

"Are you?"

"Yes, I notice that you are incredibly adept at easing conversations, at giving compliments, at saying exactly what everyone wishes to hear."

He nodded slowly, watching her.

"But where is the real Lord Featherstone? What does he want most desperately?"

He lifted his chin, a look of respect filling his face. "In you, I have found a worthy assistant."

She nearly choked. "Assistant?"

He laughed at her response and she should have been offended, but in truth, it was very difficult to be offended by Lord Featherstone. He was just so terribly delightful all the time. A person felt their very best selves when they were with him.

"Yes, assistant, or even partner, if you will. You are looking for an arrangement, are you not?"

Hesitantly, she nodded. "I had hoped Morley would take care with these kinds of conversations."

"While I respect that idea, I think it would be much more to your liking if you expressed your opinions. For example, what precisely do you want in terms of the contract?"

"Terms? Contract?"

"Yes, see, it is a contract as sure as any. Would you like anything in particular as far as your terms?"

She nodded slowly. "I've never considered things in quite this way."

"Ah, see now, I have some ideas. What if perhaps you were to be involved in a business venture of mine, earn your share of the income?"

"I . . ."

"And what if we were to have a discussion that didn't involve pin money, but more along the lines of partnering?"

She smiled but only because she didn't know what else to do. She'd never considered income or a business, except where it meant simply that she would have a warm house and food to eat and clothes to wear, something she'd gone without before and wanted to avoid ever happening again.

"And what if, my dear Miss Grace, we were to discuss the use of your dowry?"

"Lord Featherstone, this is hardly an appropriate conversation for us to be having."

"It's not? Why isn't it? I'm poised to offer you a chance to assist in the allocation of your dowry."

"Hmm."

"Probably things you've never considered before now."

"You are correct."

"Then, do give it some thought. And I will tell you why I am most interested in battling my brother for a bit of your attention."

She laughed at his jovial tone, but there was a seriousness about him that gave her pause, and made her knees go weak. Something about a man who wanted something and worked for it confidently attracted her.

"You are beautiful. And you are gentle and graceful and look the part of an extremely accomplished woman."

"Thank you, I think." He spoke as though those things did not matter.

"But what I see in you that has me strung along in your line of admirers, literally lapping up your crumbs, is ingenuity, a creativity and intelligence that is far underutilized." He spun her and when they came back together, she was a bit breathless as a result of his words.

"You . . . I've never heard someone speak as you do."

"Neither will you ever again, I'm afraid. But I speak the truth. And I would value an arrangement, a partnership, if you will."

"And children?"

His smile started slow and then grew. "I do believe that part of our relationship will grow and be wildly successful to everyone's mutual satisfaction." He grinned. "And hopefully children would result."

Her face burned with the realization of what he was saying. "You cannot say such things."

"I've said nothing. You asked about children. I merely responded that yes, they would be involved." He grinned and winked as he moved away again.

"Oh, you are too much." She spoke to the next man.

"Pardon?" He seemed taken aback.

"I am deeply sorry. I was merely responding too late to something just spoken to me."

"Sounds as though it has you ruffled." He craned his neck to see Lord Featherstone. "Ah, well, they say he's the master. He can convince any woman to do anything."

"What?"

"Certainly. He's responsible for half the marriages in the *ton* right now, so he brags. I've been considering his services myself."

Her mind spun in mad circles, thoughts racing here and there, until Lord Featherstone once again stood in front of her. All she could say was, "Your services?"

His face turned serious, and instead of making the next steps in the dance, he held out his arm. "Might we have a word?"

"Yes, I think we should."

He led her off the floor, both of them ignoring looks from anyone who might have wondered. If people were paying attention, Grace had given plenty of reason to encourage wonder and speculation in just her first ball. She caught the eye of the prince who could only raise his cup, laughter filling his face.

She looked away.

"This is going to be one interesting conversation, isn't it?"

CHAPTER 16

Oliver could not believe all that had happened in one ball. And now his brother led Miss Grace quickly from the room.

What was he up to? Oliver had half a mind to follow him. But he was also mid-set, dancing with another. To leave now would only bring scandal to Miss Grace, not to mention his current partner, and some disdain for him. He could not forget that through all this, he really was the vicar and should remain relatively scandal free. He continued asking mundane questions to a pretty redhead while focusing on his brother.

There were plenty of women in the world who had good, healthy dowries. Charles could win the hand of just about anyone. Why was he so singularly focused on Miss Grace, particularly now?

Charles was a good man. He'd encouraged Oliver to continue his own pursuit of the same woman.

Nothing made sense at the moment, and he would give

anything to be outside right now, listening in to whatever conversation was happening between the two of them.

Morley had made his way to the door. He nodded to Oliver who smiled back with gratitude. At least no supposed scandals would occur, no forced arrangements. Morley would make sure that the talk about them would be appropriate, as he himself would be witness. A person just never knew what would become scandal and what would be brushed under rugs when it came to the *ton*. Particularly at Prinny's balls, as much tended to be brushed aside, but one tongue, one wagging discontent, and a person's life could be ruined forever.

Oliver and the redhead finished up the dance. He said farewell to so many people, he lost count. Many were traveling back to London the next day. They'd come just for Prince George's ball.

He waited near the entrance of the blue room when Prince George approached. "Lord Stewart, you can expect me at your services on Sunday."

Oliver bowed. "I'm pleased to hear it."

"Say something inspiring. I'll need it after the headache from drinking too much."

"Excellent. I will, Your Highness, and might I say, thank you for your condescension."

"My pleasure. I wouldn't miss a sermon given by a man who is besotted and competing for the same woman with a brother who is also in the room. Perhaps I'll sit by the lucky lady just to ensure my grand amusement."

Oliver fought to hold his tongue. "You might find yourself surprised and distracted by the content."

"Too true. Spoken like a real vicar. Bravo!" The prince

stepped away and greeted a few of the other guests lingering and waiting for carriages.

Oliver's carriage would be next to collect him, and he still hadn't seen Morley or Miss Grace . . . or his brothers.

At last, Morley approached with a quiet Miss Grace on his arm. She looked at Oliver, held his gaze a moment and then followed Morley into their waiting carriage just ahead of his own.

Charles, George, and Jacob followed. The twins looked tired. And Charles looked calculating. That was an interesting look for him, and Oliver didn't know what to make of it. But they climbed into his carriage and relaxed into the seats.

Charles leaned his head back and closed his eyes.

Oliver watched them, but no one said anything the whole of the ride. When Charles entered the home, he moved straight to his room. But Oliver followed him.

When Oliver stepped in the room and sat on his bed, Charles groaned. "I've done enough conversing for a lifetime."

"Ah, the famous paragon tired of his act?"

He shook his head and gestured to his valet. "James."

The dutiful valet entered and loosened Charles's cravat, and he lifted one foot at a time for James. "I don't have the energy for you this evening. Just trust your brother."

"Trust you? While you're in the very act of attempting to win Miss Grace's heart?"

"It's not her heart I'm after."

"Well, her hand, then."

He dipped his head.

"That is not encouraging news."

"I don't know what to tell you. The woman will make up her mind, I'm certain, and to her own satisfaction."

"Does she know what you are, who you are?"

"She does."

This news surprised him. "You told her?"

"She heard something and figured it out mostly by herself. She's nearly as adept as I. I'm telling you, a gem."

"And she wasn't completely put off?"

"Not yet." He pulled at his cravat, finishing the work of its removal, handing a crumpled fabric to James. "Look, Oliver. I need what she says she needs. An arrangement, a partnership. We would work fabulously well together. She's just right in every way, including her dowry. From what I've heard, she is not interested in falling in love; she thinks it clouds her judgement, which is excellent by the way if we are her top two contenders." He wiggled his eyebrows. Even in fatigue the man was trying to jest.

Oliver shook his head. "But she would be much happier making decisions with her heart, especially in marriage."

"You would be. But would she? She's not certain."

"I'm certain."

Charles held out a hand, pointing directly at his chest, reminding him of the other occurrence where his finger made contact. "Then you're going to have to prove it to her because she's almost sold on the logic of my reasoning."

Alarm rushed through Oliver.

Charles closed his eyes, rubbing the back of his neck. "But she has a heart, a warm, vibrant heart."

"Of course, I know that."

"She just doesn't trust it." Charles rose and stepped

toward him, placing a hand on his shoulder. "Remember that."

"Why are we having this conversation?"

"All's fair in love and war, brother, but if she really does wish for a love alliance, then you are the best man for the job, and I want you to be happy. But if not, then you're looking at her other best option. And it would be the best for her, as well as me, in that case, believe me." His eyes held certainty, assurance, and for an odd moment, Oliver trusted that he was right. He would make an excellent life for Miss Grace.

But then Oliver shook himself out from his brother's spell. "She cannot want a life without love."

"It wouldn't be devoid of love." He placed a hand on his heart. "Do you think I wouldn't love her?"

Oliver stood up. "Anyone would love Miss Grace." As he stepped toward the door, he turned his head back over his shoulder. "But would she love you?" Then he walked out and went down the hall.

Unsettled didn't begin to explain his raging emotions. But at least his brother was playing fair. He'd laid out all the issues and even told Oliver the core obstacle. It wasn't that she didn't or wouldn't love him. It was that love wasn't enough. She didn't trust her heart.

And Oliver didn't know how to fix that.

He took to his own valet's ministrations and was at last in bed.

Sleep came slowly, even as fatigue settled in, until suddenly he was once again jerked awake. Tomorrow he had planned to pay visits to all the local area tenants. He'd done these before with the help of Miss Grace. He would certainly need her assistance again. That would work in his favor, he was certain.

With those pleasing thoughts and the remembrance of Miss Grace's lovely smile working beside him to help the poorer families, he drifted off into a deep sleep.

***

Morning came quickly. And with it, a plan for the day.

He sent off a note to the castle, asking for Miss Grace and any other hands they could spare to help deliver baskets and administer to the poor in the congregation.

Then he went about his typical morning routines. His sermon was planned, with Prince George in mind, his reading taken care of, and he even took his morning walk before he heard back from the castle.

The note was written with a feminine hand. His heart picked up. Had Miss Grace written it herself? But the words were short and to the point and . . . disappointing.

"After a ball, most are still abed. Perhaps some of the most energetic of us will join you. But I cannot guarantee any participation."

He folded the note and tucked it away. Well, no matter, he had work to do and it was a good work. He packed up his cart with all the baskets his kitchen could muster and then planned a visit to several of the homes of the more affluent in their community, asking for more.

His stops were fruitful and his cart nearly full when he decided to take a turn down the path that would lead to the castle. It was on the way to their nearest tenant, and their kitchen was always generous. He needn't even bother the family at all.

He pulled to the side of the house, near the servants'

entrance. As he approached, voices inside made him smile. Cheerful people working and doing their assigned tasks always brightened his day.

The door opened, and he had a full view of the kitchen. Miss Grace stood at its center, directing people who were refilling baskets. She turned and when she saw him, her face lit with a thousand suns.

For a moment, he was frozen in reaction to it. At last, he said simply, "Hello."

"Hello yourself. Are you ready for our baskets?"

"Yes, I am. I've got the cart just outside." He indicated to his left an almost full donkey cart.

She leaned her head backward to see where he was pointing. "Oh, that won't do. Look at what we've put together. We'll have to use ours as well." She waved to a servant. "Would you please see that our cart is ready and waiting outside this door? And quickly now, the vicar is here already and about to begin." She continued directing the others, an army of servants all about her, and Oliver saw a truly happy Miss Grace.

And the servants cared for her. They respected her, and as a result, excellence was happening.

After but a few moments, she wiped her hands on an apron and brushed some tendrils of hair from her face. "I'm afraid I'm the only person available, but I'm here. Between the two of us and the servants, I think we can help a lot of people today."

"Thank you. I'm overwhelmed as usual by your generosity. And, might I add, it is wonderful to see you, Miss Grace."

She nodded and then smiled. "I much prefer this to the ballroom."

"As do I, but dancing had its benefits, I do recall . . ." He took her hand in his and bowed gallantly, pressing his lips to her bare hands, lingering a moment longer than necessary. "Although, this right here is a wonderful distraction."

She sucked in a breath but shook her head, grinning. "This will be one interesting afternoon, won't it?"

"I'm counting on it." He tugged her hand in his. "Now, shall we ride in one cart and the servants in the other?"

"I think that would be the most useful course, yes." She laughed as he helped her up onto the wooden bench.

A line of servants began the loading of the other cart. Miss Grace looked at Oliver and then back at the servants. They both hopped down out of the cart and assisted with the loading. Soon, both carts were heavy with goods to share, and they set out down the lane.

Miss Grace sat as close as possible to him. She laughed easily and often. He could not imagine a better afternoon.

Until an all too familiar voice called out to them. "Ho there, brother."

He groaned out loud, which Miss Grace found incredibly diverting.

Oliver turned in his seat. "Yes, Charles?"

"Charles?" Miss Grace turned and shielded her eyes as she looked up at Oliver's brother. "I can see that. Charles suits you for a name."

"I'm very glad you approve because my first son will be named Charles."

She placed a finger on her chin. "Are you terribly certain?"

His hand on his heart pounded twice. "Upon my grave."

"Hmm." She frowned just a touch, enough to form a very kissable pout that Oliver found quite distracting.

Charles dipped his head. "Yes, indeed. Our first spat."

"Perhaps it shall be."

Oliver grunted. "Pardon me, brother, was there something you wanted?"

"Oh no, carry on, please. Don't stop the donkeys on my account."

Oliver recognized the mount upon which his brother sat —it was Oliver's horse. "Glad to see that Smoky is behaving for you."

"Yes, he's a brilliant mount." He rode along beside them as they dipped and shook in their cart.

Grace placed a hand on Oliver's arm and peered around him to Charles. "Will you be assisting as we deliver baskets?"

"Yes, brother, will you?" Oliver rose an eyebrow, greatly amused at the idea of his brother getting his hands dirty.

"I would love to normally, but, you see, this morning I've been invited back to the Royal Pavilion."

"No." Miss Grace widened her mouth.

"I speak the truth. Apparently, His Highness wishes for some advice in my personal expertise."

Miss Grace shook her head. "And he's married. The man has no shame."

"None whatsoever. But I must aid my country and all that, you know." He dipped his head. "I couldn't resist saying hello to two of my favorite people."

"It was lovely to see you." Miss Grace called out, waving her fingers as Charles picked up the pace slightly until he was far enough away not to shower them with dirt, then took off at a gallop.

She smiled after him. "That is an excellent horse."

Oliver quirked up the corner of his mouth. "Yes, he's been mine for ten years now."

"Does Lord Featherstone do whatever he pleases most of the time?"

"He does indeed." Oliver clucked at the donkeys.

"And he's visiting you for a time."

"Yes, precisely. I think those were the words he used. For a time."

Her mouth twitched as though she'd love to laugh, but she didn't.

Oliver could not even jest in an ill manner about his brother. "But he is a good enough man, one of the best, actually."

"I can see that."

"You can?" He turned to watch her.

"I trust him, oddly, even knowing he has such a way with people. I do believe he's giving me excellent advice and much to think about."

"Anything you would like to converse with me about?"

"No, I don't think so. Some things I need to settle in my own mind." She smiled up into his face, a lovely, caring expression. "But you are the one I wish to deliver food to the tenants with if that makes up for it."

He couldn't help but tap her on the nose. He would have done so with his lips, were they more familiar. She was simply irresistible to him. "Hmm. I'm not sure what that means about me, but I will enjoy this afternoon. I can be certain of that."

"I as well. Come, let's get this started." She took the reins from his hands and urged the donkeys on their way.

He laughed. "I have a feeling I'm just getting to know a whole new side of you."

"And I you." She eyed him and then kept her eye on their dirt path, for which he was grateful, going at the rapid speed they now were.

CHAPTER 17

race knew she was well on her way to falling in love with Lord Stewart.

She noticed every time Lord Stewart's hands brushed hers or his shoulder bumped against her or their elbows touched. And each instance sent racing sensations up her arms. She wanted to hug her middle, but then she would draw attention to her reaction.

They went over enough bumps that sent her sliding up against him that he eventually rested his arm behind her on the bench and kept her close. "That's better."

She laughed. "Thank you."

"My pleasure, believe me. And then you won't be injured bumping against me and forward and backward while we try to get down this path."

"It gets better up at the turn."

"Yes, I was just going to say that." He reached over and with her hands on the reins as well, slowed the donkeys.

At last, they arrived at the first home.

Lord Stewart paused before climbing out of the cart. "Mr. Thompson has been ill. I think he is feeling better physically, but it really hurt him in his brain somehow. He seems fully aware and converses well, but he just doesn't seem to want to leave the house anymore."

"Oh, that is so sad and hard." Her heart hurt for people in tough circumstances, especially when she knew there was no end in sight, no possible solution available. She had always had a feather of hope to lighten her own situation.

"Yes, so he hasn't been at work and they have very little to live on."

"I'm glad you told me. We could probably help."

"I'm hoping that others around them will also. Their neighbors don't have very much either, but if they help each other when in need, everyone will be better-off."

"And happier." She nodded, impressed yet again with Lord Stewart's vision.

"Yes, exactly." He lifted one of the larger baskets. "I'm happy to be able to share with them. Thank you for all of this. They can really use the extras."

"We at the castle are pleased you think of us when you are in need for things like this."

"Or *you* are, anyway. The others are still in bed." He laughed.

She laughed. "In June's defense..."

"Oh, I know. I don't fault a single one of them; it was more I, trying to praise you." He stepped closer so that their arms brushed. "I have appreciated this quality in you since we first met."

"You knew who I was?" She sucked in a breath, hardly believing such a thing.

"Of course. Just because you were the youngest doesn't mean I didn't see you. Just the opposite."

"That's embarrassing." She wiped a hair from her face. "You know I was young, uncertain, following the others around . . ."

He tipped his head back and laughed. "I have no idea why you would think so. But hold that thought. We're here." They stepped up onto the front porch and he called into the house, "Hello. It's Mr. Stewart and Miss Grace. Are you home?"

A young boy opened the door. His wide eyes and bright face made Grace smile immediately. "Well, hello! Are you Joshua?"

He nodded.

She held her hand out, measuring his new height. "Wow, you have grown. I thought for sure you were already Ned."

He giggled and someone called from inside. "No way he's me."

She cupped her mouth with one hand. "Come out here where I can see you, Ned, or I won't believe it."

A taller boy with longer hair now stood next to Joshua.

She gasped. "And you have grown like a weed. I don't even know how that happened. Has it been so long since I've been here?"

Ned rocked back and forth on his heels, thumbs in his pockets. "Not at all. You and Mr. Stewart were here last month."

She shrugged. "Then I cannot explain it. But you two must be the biggest help around here, as big as you are."

"You know they are." Mrs. Thompson joined them.

"You'll forgive us if we don't invite you in. Mr. Thompson is not feeling up to seeing visitors."

Lord Stewart shifted beside her. "Oh, I'm sorry to hear it. I was very much hoping to be able to talk to him." His kind eyes could convince anyone to do anything, Grace decided. And he now turned the full force of them on Mrs. Thompson. Sure enough, he was soon following her in.

Grace waved after them. "I'll just be out here. Maybe Ned and Joshua can help me attack some of those weeds over there."

Joshua was about to start moaning but Ned nudged him and they both led Grace over to the side of the cottage and gifted her with some gloves. Ned put a hand on his hips. "This is so you don't get your hands dirty."

"Why, thank you. I'll wear them because that is so kind of you and we are visiting lots of families today. But you remember that I'm not afraid of a little dirt, right?"

"Right."

"And you shouldn't be either. If you can get your hands dirty doing honest work, you'll be the happiest person you can be."

Ned's face turned grimmer. "Father is unhappy all the time. Says he can't work. He can't really get out of the house. Something's not right with him."

"I think he's blue. And that happens sometimes. No one really knows why, and sometimes it takes a good while for them to feel better. Sitting in the sun would sure do good for him."

The door opened, and Mr. Thompson sat on the front porch with Lord Stewart at his side. She turned to the boys with a grin.

They worked as quickly as they could, perhaps hoping that Mr. Thompson might see a little bit of their efforts and be pleased with the yard.

After a moment, Mr. Thompson's laugh carried over to the boys. Their wide eyes and hesitant smiles were so endearing, Grace had to wipe her eyes. "Do you want to go see him?"

They nodded and then hurried away, joining their father on the front porch.

Grace worked a moment more, clearing the rest of the row of weeds. There were more, but it looked much better, even ready for vegetables to be planted or spring flowers.

Mrs. Thompson brought out some biscuits from the basket for everyone on the porch, but Lord Stewart declined them. "We've just eaten, but thank you very much."

Grace made her way back to the front of the house. "The side bed looks much better, thanks to Ned and Joshua. You might even be able to plant some seeds in a couple weeks' time."

Mr. Thompson reached out and ruffled Joshua's hair. "Good work, boys. We'll plant the seeds together so your mother can have fresh carrots and potatoes, how about that?"

Mrs. Thompson's eyes turned shiny and hopeful. "I'd love some for the stew. Thank you."

After a short time more, Grace and Lord Stewart left the whole family gathered together in the sunlight on the front porch and drove on to the next family.

"That took so long, we are never going to reach everyone." Grace laughed. "But I wouldn't change a thing."

"We'll do all we can and then leave some of these with the families to deliver to each other."

"Oh, that's an excellent idea. It would help with your desire for them to be more of a community, wouldn't it?"

"I'm hoping so." He smiled, the tired wisdom she was accustomed to seeing purely visible now. "That is why I'm so pleased with the abundance of baskets that we have."

She studied him for a moment until he raised his eyebrows in question. "You know, I've always thought you were an impressive person."

"And now?" He laughed, obviously more than pleased she had such high opinions of him.

"Very funny. I still think so, of course. I just wanted you to know that you have always had my highest esteem. I want you to know that of all the men of my acquaintance, you are a most excellent choice, know this before . . ." She turned away. "Goodness, I've talked myself into an embarrassing admission."

He pulled her closer. "I like it when you're embarrassed."

"Well, that's hardly fair."

"How about this? You be embarrassed for a moment and then I will too."

Excellent. She would learn more what was going on in his head. But it would come at a cost; goodness, an embarrassing cost. She'd never talked of things to a man before about her own attractions and what not. "So, you know that I have been much impressed with you as a vicar. I take my own personal responsibility in the vicarage seriously and enjoy helping you."

He nodded. "I certainly do, one of your finest qualities, as I've said."

"But you also know that I didn't quite see you in any other way." She toyed with the ribbons on her dress. "Other than as a vicar, I mean."

"I am painfully aware, yes." He made a mock tragic expression that eased her mind somewhat.

She turned to him. "Well, then you started being more . . ."

"Handsome? Fun? Irresistible?" He winked at her but kept his eyes mostly on the path they traveled, guiding the donkeys.

She laughed. "I was going to say purposeful."

He turned to her; his mouth open. "Purposeful?" He urged the donkeys to a stop.

"Well, yes."

"That is not what I intended, I assure you."

"Oh, I know. I can guess what you intended. And it had its desired effect, believe me." She rubbed her arms. "But in your efforts to show me who you could be, to show me why they call you the Handsome Vicar, I certainly enjoyed myself." She laughed. "You're quite distracting."

"Oh? And what am I distracting you from?" He faced her, the cart paused in the shade of the trees.

Her face was close. The full force of her gaze, her eyes wide and alluring, caught his breath, as well as her soft lips. "You were distracting me from falling in love with the man I already admire."

He thought of a million things he could do in that moment. She was so close to his face, not an inch from his mouth, even. But he could not close that space. The man she admired would never take this opportunity to confuse things with a kiss. Isn't that what she was trying to say? The attraction was distracting her from falling in love with the other side of him she had been getting to know?

He did not pull away. He couldn't. It was too delicious. But he had to clear a few things up. "What are you trying to say?"

"I'm saying, let me love you, the real you, without distracting me with your other finer qualities."

HE CHUCKLED, low and soft. Grace melted in her seat at the sound, but she stayed right where she was. What would the Handsome Vicar do when presented with an opportunity to kiss her? Oh, she wanted him to. But then she didn't. How could she know for sure if she wanted to marry him if kissing became involved? She'd be lost for sure. And, of course, he hadn't asked or even indicated that he'd be interested in a courtship. Hopefully he'd talked to Morley so that he was part of the decision. Perhaps Morley would choose him and then all would be perfect in the world. Or would it? She searched his face. His lips were so close, so terribly and delightfully close. His eyes were half closed, he rested a hand on top of hers.

Lord Stewart moved closer, until she could feel his breath on her mouth. He hesitated. "Grace." The whisper filled her with warmth. She closed her eyes and then he created some space between them. His hands were trembling when he shifted the reins. "Miss Grace, that was the most difficult thing I've ever had to do."

She found her breath again and placed a hand on her racing heart. "Perhaps we should have just gone through with it."

His gaze whipped to hers. "Have you changed your mind? Might I distract you the smallest bit?"

She shook her head while she turned wide eyes to his face. "I . . . I don't know. I know what I want. But should I marry a man just because I have become needy for his touch?" She gasped and placed a hand over her mouth. "Did I just say that?"

His eyes were full of enjoyment, but not the teasing kind. And they were caring. He reached out and ran his fingers lightly over the hairs that liked to fall in her face. "I think one of the most important parts of falling in love is enjoying touch. But I won't touch you until you're ready. And remember, Miss Grace . . ."

"What?" Her voice came out far more husky than she intended, but she couldn't stop now. She was deep into her embarrassment.

"I have not as yet proposed." He leaned closer, his lips brushing her ear. "But my admission, which I'm not embarrassed about one bit, is that I plan to."

She swallowed twice before she could meet his gaze. "Am I a simpleton if I rejoice in that? If I cannot wait for the day?"

"That makes you a healthy, beautiful woman who has found someone she might want to spend her life with."

"But what if Morley doesn't pick you?"

"Morley. What does he have to do with this?"

She leaned away from him. "Everything."

"Wait. You're going to let Morley decide even now?"

"Especially now." She shook her head, her fear growing. "Especially now that I feel things. I know things. I want things." She clutched his arm. "How can I make a good decision when all I want to do is see what it feels like to kiss you?" She turned from him. "You must think me in great need of confession."

He was quiet for a long time before he reached for her hand. "I wish you didn't think of me as *your* vicar."

"But you are." She faced him again. "Am I so unholy?"

He sighed. "You are not."

"But the church—"

"A man is commanded to leave his family and cleave unto his wife. Marriage is good. Families, children, all godly things. So I feel that this feeling, this closeness we have, is holy too, one of the most holy things you would ever do."

She sat back in her seat. The power of their almost-kiss still rushing through her. "And that's your opinion as my vicar or as a man?"

He laughed and held out his hands. "Unfortunately, I am both." He raised her hand to his lips. "Or perhaps *fortunately,* as you tend to enjoy the man in me, or am I mistaken?"

"Do I enjoy you being a man? Oh, I enjoy it." She laughed at herself. "Who would have guessed that I'd have such passion and wish to communicate it?" She turned from him and mumbled, "Or wanton."

"Say no such thing. I'm more pleasantly surprised than you would ever be able to guess." They approached the next house. "But I will tell you that we are now at great odds with one another."

Concern flickered in her stomach until she saw the light dancing in his eyes. "Oh, and how is that?"

"You insist that I not muddy your thinking with efforts to be near you, to touch you, to kiss you."

"I would appreciate that, yes."

"Yet I vow to make it my life's goal to do exactly that."

She breathed out in amazement. "Oh, I think I'm going to enjoy this far too much."

When he did not laugh at her open admission but kissed her hand again, she loved him all the more. How was she ever going to be able to decide? She couldn't.

And that is why Morley better make the right choice. A life with someone as wonderful as Lord Stewart would be a joyful life indeed.

CHAPTER 18

Oliver finished one of the most enjoyable days of his life with a smile that could not be dimmed. His brothers made so much fun at his expense, they were all rolling with laughter in his study that night before bed.

"And so you've at last kissed the woman?" Charles raised his glass in salute.

Oliver shook his head.

Charles lowered his glass. "Are you daft?"

"I am not daft. It's complicated, as you know. She doesn't want her decision distracted by the physical aspects of our attraction."

"But there is attraction." His perceptive eyes searched Oliver's like a physician seeking a cure.

"I thought the cart would catch fire."

"Excellent." Charles downed his drink. "I shall keep up my efforts."

"I do not know why you persist." Oliver breathed out while placing his cup aside.

"I have my reasons."

"You cannot win when she asks for kisses from me."

"She *asked*, and you did not comply." His eyebrow was so far up in his hairline, it appeared ridiculous.

Charles's incredulity gave rise to a great feeling of unease. "I don't expect you to understand."

"You are correct. I do not understand. She's going to think of this almost kiss as a rejection. You know that."

"I do not."

"Then, you do not know women."

"I don't think of them in the same way you do. But I was presented with a woman who acted as though she wanted to be kissed, but in the very act of doing so, she also told me it would confuse her." He leaned back against his desk. "I think I made the right choice."

"But all night long, she will be plagued with insecurities about you. 'Why didn't he kiss me?' will repeat a thousand times in her mind, and do you know what she will come up with for an answer?"

"What?" Oliver could not take his eyes off his brother.

"That you obviously don't care for her. That you are her vicar. That you have determined she is unworthy and wanton."

He felt his own face go white. "No. Do you think she will think those things?"

"I am almost certain of it. Unless she is more confident than any woman of my acquaintance."

"She is not." Oliver knew her to be overly unsure of herself in regard to men, which was why she had asked for this whole arrangement of a marriage in the first place. "What have I done?"

"I don't know. But the opportunity to kiss a woman is a rare gift indeed. You might not get another chance."

He knew Charles was correct. Had he been gifted a beautiful blessing and let it slip away?

George and Jacob laughed their way to their rooms. Charles patted him on the back. "You might have had her vote, but you know I have Lord Morley's." With those further-deflating words, his older brother left him alone to his pondering.

What a mess he was in. He should have known that marrying a woman would be fraught with confusion, missteps, and despair. Why could he not flirt with a woman, ask to court her, then marry her? Was that not how it was done over and over for a thousand years?

He needed a new plan, and he needed one right away.

Nothing came to him and his frustrations grew.

But he certainly had a few new ideas for his sermon on Sunday. If he didn't shock half the congregation, at least he'd give them some important things to think about. The corner of his mouth lifted. And Prince George, who had promised to attend, would certainly enjoy this sermon above all else, until he hated it.

Oliver laughed to himself. The man might never return. And that was just fine with Oliver.

He was about to make his way to his bed when a servant came rushing in. "Mr. Wilson at the door, Mr. Stewart. He dares not come in, says his family has the plague."

Oliver's stomach sank. "Tell him I'll be right there. Has the physician been called?"

"I don't know."

"Find out and call him if he hasn't."

169

"Yes, sir."

Oliver rushed to his room, donned his most practical clothing, grabbed a few necessities, and ran from the house.

Mr. Wilson stayed a good distance away, but Oliver called him over. "I will be entering your home. I'll be doing what I can to assist the physician. No need to keep your space."

"Thank you, Mr. Stewart, but please don't be getting yourself ill. A prayer is all we need. We shall be well with a prayer." As he spoke, he doubled over in pain, vomiting all over his boots.

"There now, let's get you home and then all washed up, shall we?"

"I'm afraid there's no one to do the washing."

"Are you all sick?"

"Every last one of us, myself included. It came on fast. We didn't want to get the neighbors infected."

"You're a good man. I'm glad someone came to fetch help at last."

The two hurried as quickly as they could, Mr. Wilson stumbling to keep his balance, until they at last arrived at the cottage.

The stench alone when Oliver opened the door was enough to make any man vomit. "First we must air out the whole place." He left the door open.

What he saw in that cottage was beyond what any person should have to see in their lifetime. He began immediately lugging things out of the doors. He piled them high in the middle of the yard and everything with a bit of fabric in it was promptly caught on fire. "I'm sorry, Mr. Wilson. I hope nothing here is more valuable than your lives."

"Not at all." He fell into a chair. "I'll help. I just need a moment." He closed his eyes and then slid to the floor.

Oliver ran to him, laying him out flat. He would get him a place to rest when he made a clean space.

He worked without stopping, throwing out piles of blankets and clothing and rugs, watching them burn over his shoulder while he cleared out the home. Mrs. Wilson and children were huddled together on a bed. He left them be for now.

Then he emptied all their water buckets, scouring them out with what kinds of soaps he could find.

He took to scrubbing the floors, the tables, the bedposts, everything he could imagine had been touched by the effects of cholera, which is what this looked to be.

Hours later, when at last the place seemed to smell better—or perhaps he was merely accustomed to it—he began to think of food. Or water to drink.

He'd dug up the last of the Wilson's blankets in a cupboard. Mrs. Wilson and her two children were feverish and shivering together. Mr. Wilson was moved to some ticking on the floor nearby.

Oliver went to go get water from the well.

The doctor arrived when he was lugging the water back up to the house.

"Mr. Stewart." He nodded, his tired eyes telling a sad tale.

"Hello, Mr. Green. Are you well?"

"As well as can be. It's spreading. Down by the river, all the people live close together, some in tents, do you know the place?"

"I don't, I'm ashamed to say."

"Most don't like to remember it exists. But illness spreads there like nowhere else. I think we have it under control but not before there is significant loss."

"I'm sorry." He led Mr. Green into the bedroom.

"Someone's been working hard in here." He nodded with approval. "We've found the disease is carried through the waste. You've done good to clear it out and burn it."

"Thank you. I was just hoping to alleviate the smell."

"Your instincts served you well. Now, let's have a look at our patients."

Oliver left him to the family while he took to cleaning the dishes and seeing what could be made for a bite to eat. He was not at all accustomed to work in the kitchen. He'd never attempted to make much more than a boiled egg. The Wilsons didn't have much. But he did find a half a loaf of bread. That would probably suit more than anything else anyway.

But to begin, water. He brought in a fresh bucket of water with a ladle.

"Excellent. The more they drink, the better. I don't know if they're ready to eat, except perhaps this young one."

The young girl sat up, and with a shaky hand, took the ladle. She drank. "Might I have more?"

"Certainly." He gave her ladle after ladle until she laid back down.

"Are you hungry?"

She nodded and so he broke off a healthy chunk of the loaf, which she began to eat slowly.

Oliver smiled at her.

The doctor breathed out in relief. "Well, we have one of them back. Let's work on the others."

He left a list of instructions for Oliver.

"They don't have much by way of food. I'll see if I can get some help . . ."

The doctor shook his head. "We aren't sure how it spreads besides the filth. You cannot be in contact with others."

"Surely I could call from the lawn."

"You could, but please don't spread this any further. It is wiping out families."

Oliver swallowed. "Understood. Would you mind leaving a message at my home?"

"Do you really want me going to your home?"

He then shook his head rather adamantly. "Point taken. How long until I know if I'm contagious or if I will get it?"

"If you are careful and don't touch your mouth, you might not catch it. But I cannot be certain how long it takes. I'm sorry, Mr. Stewart. You're a good man and have just walked into a trying situation."

Oliver sighed. "I'd rather be a good man in a trying situation than a weak man who does nothing."

"And that's why we love you. Thank you, Mr. Stewart. And don't forget, prayers do wonders."

He wiped his brow. "Prayer is the reason I was called here, and I haven't yet begun."

"Sometimes we need to do the work we can first, I believe."

"That's understandable as a physician. Thank you for reminding me."

"I will be making my way, but if other cases pop up, at least you know how to treat it." With that, he tipped his hat to Oliver and walked out the door.

Had he just left Oliver in charge of an entire street full of tenant families who might get this horrible disease?

Surely there was a way to get word to his brothers at least. To Miss Grace.

A moan came from the back room, and he hurried there.

He'd learned from the physician some methods of washing the remaining blankets so that they would not spread the disease. So after cleaning up multiple times after the Wilson's and washing bedding and hanging it all to dry, he thought his knuckles might never be the same. He stood in their doorway, a breeze still blowing through the home to keep the air clean, and at last began a prayer.

It was simple, heartfelt, and short. Then he found a corner of the floor he was reasonably certain was clean, curled himself up in a ball, and fell asleep. He heard nothing, felt nothing, thought nothing, until a hazy sound interrupted his blessed silence. It was muffled, far away, but would not stop.

Crying.

Children crying.

He forced himself to sit up, rubbing his face, then realized he was covered in something, something abhorrent. A child sat over him, using a bit of fabric to wipe her face.

He used a clean portion of his sleeve to wipe his own nose and mouth, then lifted the child and began the process of cleaning all over again.

That was the beginning of his quick road to infection. He knew it the minute his stomach started churning.

The next day Mrs. Wilson was at least sitting up.

He gave her the instructions he'd received from the

doctor, told her alarmed face that he would be leaving, told her to alert the neighbors, and then walked out the door.

He waved to some as he hurried from the house, down the lane, through back pathways and bits of forest until he found what he was looking for: an old hunter's cabin. He had no idea who owned it or who's property he was on, but he'd seen it before and knew it to be uninhabited with a well out front.

He pumped the well, fighting back the urge to vomit, and laughed in relief when water came pouring out.

He held his head under that precious clear water, then his chest. Next he filled a bucket that he dumped on himself, causing a great cold to come upon him, but he welcomed the cold. It was fresh and clean. He scrubbed his body, his face, rinsed out his mouth, scrubbed his arms, anything and everything he could scrub, and then went inside in search of another bucket.

On the way, he lost all the contents of his stomach.

A great shiver rose from the core of his body.

And that's when he knew he was in trouble.

It took every bit of strength he had left to rinse out a dusty old bucket and fill it also with water.

He slopped his dripping, shivering self, back into the dusty, musty old cabin, fell onto a wooden pallet, and drifted back off to sleep.

CHAPTER 19

*G*race enjoyed Lord Featherstone. He shared quip after joke after interesting, pleasant detail. But what she loved most about him were his stories of Lord Stewart.

"You know, Oliver was the most precocious of us all as a lad."

"What? I cannot believe it. The most precocious Stewart becomes a vicar?"

"Isn't that always the way? No, he really was. But he got in trouble for all the right reasons."

"How can you get in trouble for right reasons?"

"Well, the cat in the tree, for example."

She laughed. "He did not rescue a cat."

"Oh, he did, but he didn't climb up after it. He shook the tree and threw rocks near it."

She nodded, unsure how to feel about this story.

"Until the cat became so dissatisfied with his situation

and he left on his own. That's the only way, you know. Cats, they stay up there forever until they choose."

"I suppose most living things wish to choose." She sighed and looked away.

"You *can* trust your feelings, you know." Lord Featherstone murmured the words so that no one else would hear. "You are an excellent judge of character."

"You're just saying that because I prefer your company above many."

"It does influence my opinion of you in your favor, of course, but take me seriously this once. Trust yourself."

"Hmm." She toyed with a bit of fabric on her skirts. She'd love to tell Lord Featherstone of her wanton ways. But he would only lose interest, just as Lord Stewart appeared to have done. "Do you know where he is?"

"He left two nights ago. That's all anyone knows. Oh, and something about a sickness here abouts was mentioned." Lord Featherstone flicked his fingers as though it didn't matter.

She shook her head. "But he should be back. Surely praying with a family would not take all this time."

"I cannot say. He hasn't sent word except to warn people away and that was within the first day from a lad who wasn't to come near the house. I didn't receive the message. Apparently it was highly convoluted."

She pretended to be satisfied with that answer. They talked and made light and enjoyed an outside tea with shuttlecock and other lawn games. But Grace's head was far away.

She'd spent most of the night concerned. She'd practically thrown herself at Lord Stewart. She'd poured her wanton desires at his feet; only, he hadn't responded. They hadn't lost themselves in reckless abandon, because he had held himself in check. He'd been a gentleman.

She daren't guess what he must think of her now.

And he'd disappeared soon after.

The afternoon promised to be full of angst and concern if she didn't hear from Lord Stewart soon.

Kate and Lord Dennison strolled down the lawn.

Grace leapt from her chair, grateful beyond measure for something else to do. She wrapped her arms around her sister. "I'm so pleased you have come."

"I hear we're to choose your husband this weekend."

"Are we?" She glanced over her shoulder at Lord Featherstone who surely must have heard but pretended to be deaf. "Come meet a determined contender."

"Determined?" Kate laughed. "My."

"Yes, he's perfect. You'll think so after about ten minutes in his company."

"Lord Featherstone?" She smiled and held out her hand to greet him. "He and I are old friends."

"In a manner of speaking, we are. I'm not certain it was her intent, but a timely caricature of myself and a few words penned by her notorious column, *Whims and Fancies*, has given me more clients than I'd ever care to admit."

"Ah, so you know him and . . . everything."

"Yes, I do." Kate's expression did not give Grace any hint as to her feelings on the matter. Kate turned to more fully face Lord Featherstone. "And now you've come seeking my sister's hand?" She studied him for many moments. "It could be an excellent match."

"You can see that?" Grace gripped her arms. "You

already know such a thing? This is my life we're talking about here." A certain panic rose up inside her.

"Take care, sister. I'm not dooming you to a life with an ogre. Lord Featherstone is an excellent chap."

He dipped his head, lowering his hat in a gallant and grand gesture. "Thank you, high praise indeed."

Grace looked from one to the other, not entirely understanding their relationship, but she was pleased for her sister to be back in town. "But we shan't be flippantly making decisions either, correct?"

"Of course not. Besides, some of these things only take a matter of moments." She linked arms with Grace, a large smile filling her face.

"Moments? Surely not. Great care, excellent careful study is involved." Grace's indignation rose.

"Hmm. I suppose." She tugged her closer. "Come, you must best me in shuttlecock yet again."

They finished up their lawn games, and Lord Featherstone left them in peace. Except that Grace felt anything but peace. She didn't think her family members were taking their role of arranging her marriage seriously enough.

A meeting up in June's room was immediately called. Morley stood at the top of the stairs. "Please join us. We have exciting news to discuss."

Morley brought in extra chairs, and Grace sat on June's bed. "How are you, dear sister?"

"The doctor said I'm almost able to move about again. It's time for this baby to come and so I don't need to be so careful. Just another week or two is all."

"That is the best news." She squeezed June's hand. "I cannot wait to meet our new member of the family."

"Or I, believe me." Her brow wrinkled and her eyes looked tired.

In all of Grace's confusion, she had not thought enough about her sister. "Are you truly well though?"

"I'm well enough. Some good sunshine would be an excellent remedy for what ails me." She sighed and her eyes wandered to the window.

Grace stood. "We must take this meeting out of doors."

"But...June." Morley turned tender eyes to his wife.

"Your June needs fortification. She is about to have a child and she needs fresh air and the sun." She reached for June's hand. "Come. Morley can carry you and the rest of us would be just as happy in the sun as here."

"Agreed." Lucy stood.

"Or the courtyard. We could sit there." Morley suggested a compromise of sorts.

"Certainly. That is just the place. In that comfortable chair we keep by the fire." June's voice was soft but held a rising hope that made Grace smile.

Morley called for the servants, and in a matter of minutes, June was being carried down the stairs and a meeting gathered in the courtyard.

"We will be heard." Grace looked around them, knowing how well sound carried to every servant in the house.

"Do you think they don't already know the details for our lives?" Kate laughed.

"But this is *my* particular life. Did you want everyone knowing the details of your pre-marriage situation?"

Kate's face colored, remembering perhaps how she had tried to keep her authorship a secret. "You are correct. But is there something you wish to tell us that is perhaps more sensitive in nature?"

She thought of all the things she could say, but then shook her head. She was planning to say as little as possible. "Mostly I want to listen. I've asked you all to do a very important, very special thing for me, and I'm trusting you will give it your best efforts, your best thoughts, and all your love to help me be happily married to a good and safe man."

Everyone returned her gaze but didn't seem to be as touched as she would like. "Are you taking this seriously?"

"Yes, Grace. What more do you want? We are all gathered to help you decide." The voice came from behind. *Charity.*

Grace whipped around. "You came!" She ran to her sister and threw her arms around her neck. "You are the most forthright. Thank you."

Morley smiled at them all. "Now that we are all present, I would like to let you all know what has been done thus far. I've asked three gentlemen to come visit us in Brighton so that we might get to know them better. Two immediately fell out of my good graces. We don't even need to mention their names. But one is by far the best chap of any of my acquaintance to this point. I know much is said of Lord Featherstone, but I find that in my interactions with him and while watching him with our Grace, he is a man a notch above the others. He is jolly, friendly, caring, and must be good. How could he not be, as the brother of our exceptional vicar?" He shifted in his seat to glance at June who seemed as pleased as anything to be sitting in a chair.

"We can spend more time on this. We can meet more men, or attend more events, but from what I've seen already,

I'd be happy to stop right here and invite Lord Featherstone to be a member of our family."

Grace bolted to her feet. "Wait, that's it? Has no one else spoken with you?" She felt her face drain of life, her hands went cold. She sat again. Had Lord Stewart not asked Morley for her hand, had he not said anything?

"Is there someone else we should consider?" Morley's kind eyes sought her out. "Is there a secret love somewhere that must make his way to ask for your hand?" He chuckled and reached for June's.

Grace waved her hand. "No. I mean, of course not. These are the things I want you to work out among yourselves. I could never make this choice or encourage a man or . . . decide." She swallowed. The words came out in a great mumble. Lord Stewart was missing. He'd said nothing to Morley. He'd refused to kiss her when given a chance. He must not care. He was friendly, even flirtatious. But he did not care? She could hardly believe it. She stood again. "I have to go."

"Wait, Grace." June's soft voice followed her out the door, but she didn't turn back. She ran down the lane toward the vicarage.

She had no idea what she would do when she got there, but she had to know what Lord Stewart wanted. She had to know what he thought of her.

A persistent voice nagged at her with the reminder that if he cared he would have asked Morley for her hand.

But he hadn't.

He'd also told her in no uncertain terms that he was going to court her, that he planned to propose.

But he hadn't.

Instead, he'd disappeared and said nothing to Morley or her since.

She had to know. Her family was about to marry her to Lord Featherstone. She had to know before she agreed to such a thing.

When she arrived at the vicarage, she was stunned at the crowd of people standing in the front green and pouring into the house.

And every person there was a woman.

Young women with their mothers, older women with their young ones. So many women filled the space around in front of his home. She approached the first group. "Excuse me. What is happening here?"

"Oh, Mr. Stewart isn't home. We've all come for our counseling with him, and he isn't here. No one knows when he will be back." The woman brought a handkerchief to her eye.

"You're all here to counsel with him?"

She nodded. "I am. He helps me feel so much better about things."

Grace narrowed her eyes at the gathering. All these women were here to see Lord Stewart?

She politely shifted her step so that she might squeeze in and around others to make her way inside the door. Mrs. Gibbons would know. Surely someone knew where he was.

The woman bustled here and there, offering tea or water to some, fanning herself and shifting items around so as to make room for more people. When she saw Grace, her face lit in flash of relief. "Oh good, you're here. I can use the help, I'll tell you that."

"Please tell me what has happened."

THE FOIBLES AND FOLLIES OF MISS GRACE

Mrs. Gibbons led her back to the servants' part of the house, through the kitchen and into the tiniest of offices. She leaned against the wall. "We need help from the castle." She wiped her face.

"What is it? Where is Lo—Mr. Stewart? Where are his brothers?"

She shook her head. "They've gone out to find him."

"Find him?" Grace's heart began to pound.

"Yes, he's not returned, not since visiting the Williamses'."

"How long has that been?"

"Three days?"

"And the Williamses? Do they know where he is?"

"They don't. They had the cholera. Almost didn't make it. The doctor saw Mr. Stewart, said he was cleaning their house, feeding them by himself." Her face constricted. "If only I had known . . . But he left there. Walked out the back, and no one has seen him since. Everyone, Dr. Green especially, warned us not to go on that street, to stay far away from the Williamses'."

Grace's heart constricted. "And the brothers are out looking? By this house?"

"Yes, I think so. Within reason. The whole village had cholera. It's not safe to enter the houses. He could be anywhere, helping any of them . . . he could be sick himself." She gripped Grace's arms. "What are we to do?" Her eyes were stricken.

Grace pulled her into a hug. "For one, you are going to rest." When she could see the woman was about to fight her, Grace shook her head. "I'll take care of these people. And have more tea and food sent over from the castle."

"Oh, that would be lovely. I'm strong. I can do many things, but this . . ." She wiped her forehead again.

"Are you well?"

"I . . . don't know." She swayed in place and then swooned into Grace's arms.

"Someone come quickly!"

A servant from the kitchen opened the door. "Oh my stars! Oh goodness!" She wrung her hands and looked as though she'd begin to wail.

"Stop right now." Grace shifted under the weight of Mrs. Gibbons. "You will help me lower her safely to the ground first before you begin crying."

The servant nodded and reached out.

When Mrs. Gibbons was on the floor in the hall, Grace took a deep breath. "We need a manservant to bring her to her bed. We need a doctor, but not Dr. Green. And we need a message sent to the castle. We need food for your kitchens."

"Yes, miss."

"What is your name?"

"Abigail."

"Excellent. I need for you to get ready to be cooking a large amount of food."

"Yes, miss."

Grace exited to the front room.

Most everyone ignored her. They were carrying on and gossiping and supposing so many things that Grace had about lost her patience with the lot of them.

"Excuse me."

Only a few turned curious eyes in her direction.

"Friends. Friends. Friends." By the third friends she was speaking rather loudly and many had stopped to listen.

"Thank you for giving me your attention. We have several announcements to make. The first is, our village has been hit with cholera."

Everyone began carrying on and talking loudly.

Grace raised her hands and called out. "There's more."

They quieted. "We need you to assist where you can in these homes. But be aware. It is highly contagious. Please leave your help at the doors. Ask from the front of the house what more they need. Do what you can without getting sick."

"Where is Mr. Stewart?" A small, frail sort of woman called out from the back.

"He has gone to help. We are not sure when he will be coming back. But we are going to need you to leave the vicarage. There is nothing to do here. Please go be of assistance to our neighbors and spread the word. This is a safe house for those in true need. We will have food and shelter for all those who are desperate. The rest of you, solve your problems by reaching out to another household."

The noise picked up, but the people started leaving. Word was spread to all those on the lawn. Grace watched it spread from person to person like a great wave of doom. She hoped they would lift a hand. She hoped they would assist. She hoped they would leave. To think this group had brought the housekeeper to faint under the load of attempting to attend to them.

As soon as the front room was empty, she returned to Mrs. Gibbons. With any luck, she did not have cholera.

CHAPTER 20

Oliver awoke, unsure where he was. There was very little light, and his head ached. He shifted his body and groaned. He was on a cold hard floor. His shoulder and hip might never be the same. As he sat up and the cloud in his brain began to clear, he started to remember all the things that lead up to his being where he was. He jerked to his feet and then wobbled; the world spun and started to gray.

"No!" he cried, grabbing his head. With one hand, he gripped his knee. "Do not faint."

His vision started to clear. He took deep breaths and slowly raised himself up. The cabin was small. It smelled of years of dust and unuse. The water bucket was still full. He put his whole face in the water, gulping it down. A dry and cracked throat welcomed the cool liquid. Then he washed his face, rubbed his hands.

His clothes were dry and crinkly. He'd been sopping wet when he'd entered. How long had he been asleep? He ran some water through his hair, brushed down his clothing and then slowly made his way to the door.

As he creaked it open, bright sunlight through budding trees shone down in his eyes. He squinted and lifted a hand to shield him from the pain that sliced through his head. Was he sick? He blinked furiously and at last could see clearly in the brightness of day.

He had to make his way home. But not by way of the village. Too much sickness there. He could go home and sleep in the barn if he felt ill. No one would catch the sickness from him there. As he walked, one foot in front of the other, he could only be amazed at what a terrible illness that had shaken the Williamses. Hopefully they were well. He knew that poor mother must have had a terrible time of it when he left, she having just barely recovered, but there was nothing for it. He had been ill, desperately so, or so he felt. But now, he felt nothing but fatigue. If he could have but a soft place to lay his head, he might sleep for days.

After a long walk, the kind that felt like a journey through the desert, he at last pushed open the door to his barn. His horse knickered at him. "Hey, boy. Any space in here for me?" He reached a hand up to caress his horse's nose, then he lowered himself to the ground at the door in front of his stall and leaned his head back against it. "I'll just rest here a moment."

When he opened his eyes again, it was to a noise outside the door. His brothers? He reached a hand down to lift himself up. He pushed open the door into the yard to see an extremely disheveled Charles who was making a caterwauling kind of noise.

Oliver leaned against the aging wood while he tried to understand what he was seeing.

Charles, who looked like he hadn't slept in days, paced about. "No, he's not anywhere. He could be in any of those houses helping who knows how many sick and dying people, or he could be on a deathbed himself with no one giving him an ounce of attention. We've looked the place over ourselves, and now we need the magistrate. We need His Grace. Get the prince down here. I don't care what or who we call, find someone to find my brother before he leaves the earth . . ."

Oliver waved his hand, but no one saw him.

Charles was shouting toward the house and no one had as yet exited to attend to him. Jacob and George were walking away from him, or rather dragging their feet. All three looked like they the plague itself. They looked like he felt. He tried to wave his hand again. "Charles."

But his voice was so powerless. He was so weak.

Then the door opened and the person he most wanted to see in all the world stepped out. It was as if the sun itself had begun shining from its stoop. "Lord Featherstone?" She gazed with confusion at him, but her eyes immediately shifted to Oliver.

Her face contorted into a sorrowful joy, the kind of look he hoped to never see her express again. She rushed to him.

Charles was shortly behind her and soon he was squished and upheld by two sets of strong arms, one soft and one firm.

Her tears wet his shirt anew. His own tears fell without bother. Charles's eyes were level with his. "Brother."

"I am well. I think."

"We feared the worst." Charles's voice shook.

"I did not." Her muffled voice came from down at his chest; that she was in between the two brothers made him smile.

They separated, but Charles kept an arm around Oliver, holding him up.

"Oh, you didn't?" Oliver couldn't take his eyes off Grace's face.

She shook her head. "No. We've got things all ready for when you would arrive. It's been quite a task, with Mrs. Gibbons abed and the rest of the house catching fevers." She caught her breath. "But the kitchen is active and running. We've been feeding all who come. The front room may be a mite difficult to navigate. I only used that door because Lord Featherstone was making such a fuss that he was waking the children." She tsked at Charles and then led them to the side entrance. "This will be much better. We've reserved your quarters and your study for your personal use. It should be quiet and cool in there." She opened the door and held it for him.

But he couldn't move. Charles started their steps, but he held up a hand to pause them. Oliver's throat felt full with emotion. He choked out, "You've done all this?"

"Of course." Her lips wavered. "When you could not be here, someone had to help the flock." Tears filled her eyes. "I have missed you terribly. I hope I've done things . . . correctly." She looked as though she might crumple herself, suddenly in great need of encouragement.

Oliver pulled her into an embrace, finding new strength as he held her tight and close, then kissed the top of her head. "You are the angel I've always said you are. You are

everything we needed right when we needed it. Thank you."
He kissed her head again.

Then Charles tugged him away. "And you smell like the barn."

"Oh! Do I?" He smiled. "I don't suppose I noticed."

Charles sniffed and then placed a hand over his nose. "Believe me, the rest of us did."

"You don't smell any better I'd imagine." He nudged him with his shoulder.

"Perhaps not. But let's get you inside, nonetheless."

Oliver reached for Grace's hand. "I love you."

She choked and then tears fell anew. "I love you too."

"And there goes my chance." Lord Featherstone flicked his fingers. "Out the window. Like the birds."

"Oh hush. You never had a chance." Oliver wrapped an arm around his brother as they entered the house together. Before they turned out of sight, he looked back at Grace. She watched them, her eyes smiling, her face full of happiness. She was a wonder. She'd done all this while he was incapable. Of course she had. He tried to say I love you again, but Charles tugged him back. "She knows already. She knows."

Her laugh carried to him, and that was enough.

Charles shook his head. "Brother. Where have you been?"

"The Williamses were sick. I don't know. I went to a shack sort of place where I wouldn't spread the dreaded thing."

And then Charles vomited all over him.

"Charles." He lifted his face. It was green, and his eyes foggy. "Oh dear, no." He called out. "Someone!"

A man he didn't recognize stepped in his door immediately entering his bed chambers. "Mr. Stewart."

"Lord Featherstone is ill. Could you help me get him into my bed?"

"Yes, right away."

"And when you're finished, wash yourself with lye."

"Yes, sir."

They both lifted him and laid him on the most welcome sight Oliver had seen in a long time. His own bed. He dismissed the other fellow and stripped his brother of his soiled clothing, replacing it with night clothes, crisp and fresh from his wardrobe. Then he covered him and placed a cool cloth on his forehead. "Sleep, brother. It is the best way to get through this."

"Sorry that you did this all by yourself."

"It was for the best. Now sleep."

More servants he didn't recognize started carrying in water for a bath, and he didn't complain one bit. Soon he was soaking all the dirt, grime, and germs off his body, all while attempting to form some kind of thought. It was too difficult to make much sense of anything, except he loved Grace, and she loved him. And that was all he needed to know right now.

He sunk down into the warm water, letting the last of its warmth soak into him as deeply as it would go and then he stood.

His valet showed up out of nowhere.

"Goodness, man. You startled me."

"I'm sorry, m'lord. I just learned you had returned."

"You're calling me lord now?"

"Miss Grace informed me of your title."

"And if I say it is unnecessary?"

"She told me to tell you that I would be doing you a disservice to call you anything other than your title."

"And therefore, you will persist."

"I will, m'lord."

"Very well, can we get some lordly-looking clothes on me, then?"

"Certainly." He smiled. "I've been learning the latest cravat styles."

"Have you?"

"Yes, I think if you will be using your title, you should dress as a lord. Might help the congregation as well."

"Do you think it would?"

"Certainly. They might increase their donations and might start helping each other more, that sort of thing."

"And the women?"

"Well, Miss Grace has made them all leave."

"She has?" His grin grew, wondering how that conversation happened.

"Yes, she told them to come if they wanted to be of use, otherwise be of use to those who really need the help."

"Excellent."

"I thought so as well."

Oliver's grin grew. "So, you've taken to Miss Grace, have you?"

"She's what kept this place going if I may say so."

"You may. I will always be pleased to hear praise of Miss Grace."

"Everyone loves her. The servants and the nobles alike. She is an angel."

"An angel. She is, isn't she?"

She is also a woman, if he remembered correctly, a woman desiring to be kissed, a soft, vibrant, smart woman who teased and flirted. He smiled to himself. Angels could be women too.

And pleased he was for it.

"Now, let's see if I might take a tour of the house."

"Oh, I'm sorry, m'lord, but the instructions are that you are to wait for a tray for dinner and then sleep here in the study."

"My . . . study?"

"Yes, they will have brought bedding in there for you and pushed the desk aside."

Oliver could only shake his head. "Might I guess this is also the doing of Miss Grace?"

"It is, yes. She's keeping us together, like I said."

He rubbed his face. "I can only hope my brother will be well when he wakes."

"The doctor has been called."

"Excellent."

He stepped into his study to find Grace, placing the tray on his desk, which had indeed been moved aside so that he could take his rest.

Her soft face was as welcome as early sunshine. And he let it soak a peace and warmth into him like he'd never felt before.

"In the morning I've arranged for you to move to the castle if you'd like. There is a whole wing in the family section where you could recover in almost-isolation, except for food at your door if you're still ill. Are you?" She searched his face, stepping closer. "You look much better after your bath."

He pulled her close and held her in a hug. "I'm past the worst of it."

"You smell much better too."

"Can you ever forget me in that state? I don't imagine it was an attractive sight."

"I cared not one whit how you looked—I was so happy you'd been found. And that you were on your feet." She shook her head against him. "I've been so worried." The face she turned up to his was the one she had kept hidden earlier. It was tired, stricken with worry, and concerned. He brushed aside her hair. "I've heard that you've kept everything going over here."

"I don't know, but I did what I thought you'd like to be done and prepared for when you would come back. I prayed and prayed." Her eyes welled again. "And here you are. I cannot thank God enough for this blessing. I don't even care who I marry, as long as you are well and here. You can be my vicar all my days and I will be satisfied."

He frowned. "Oh no, you won't." He tapped her nose. "Let's hear none of that."

"That was my agreement with God. If He just brought you back, I'd be satisfied with whatever became of my life."

"And what if your life is meant to be full and joyful and passionate? Do you want to sit on your pew and only imagine kissing the vicar?"

She snorted. "You did not just say such a thing to me right now."

"Oh, I did." He started to laugh and then laughed harder and couldn't stop until his own tears joined hers. "I love you, Grace. Be my wife. Would you like this life? It's not glamorous. But it's important. And you're so good at it, but it's more than that. I love you. I want you at my side forever, through all of it, the balls and the sicknesses. Is this a good enough life for you?" He paused, knowing he was not selling himself in quite the way that Charles would have done it.

She smiled, her grin growing larger the more he spoke. "Hold that thought."

"What? How can I hold this thought? It's the most important question of my life."

"I know. And I want you to ask me again in front of all my family."

He groaned. "Still your family must be involved?"

"They must. Please understand me in this."

"I will try."

She nodded, then stepped up on her toes and whispered, "Do you know what I'll say?" She was so close, so kissably close, that he almost did not resist. Instead, he murmured against her lips. "Do you want me to kiss you right now?"

She paused, ran her lips against his, the barest brush and then created more distance. "Not. Yet."

He closed the distance she created. "I want you to know that every time I resist, I grow more earnest in my desire to press my lips against yours, wetting them with my own again and again until neither of us can breathe." He breathed out his yearnings with his forehead against hers.

She nodded, licking her mouth, catching her breath. "That is something to look forward to then, isn't it?"

"Yes, it is. When is this meeting with your family?"

"I was hoping three days ago, but Morley had heard nothing of your desire to marry me." She put her hands on her hips. "I didn't want to bring it up, you just having arrived and without a bed and a house full of strangers, but it was something I noticed."

He pulled out a paper and quill. "I shall take care of that oversight this instance."

"Oh, very good. Thank you. That will help things along."

He shook his head. Then he took her hand and pressed his lips against it as fiercely as he could, lingering as long as he could. She slid her fingers away and walked out the door.

Charles called from the other room. "Good show, brother. I've taught you well."

"Go to sleep."

He just moaned in response while Oliver drafted a most important, short, and to-the-point letter to Lord and Lady Morley.

CHAPTER 21

*G*race was more exhausted than she'd ever felt. When she made it upstairs to the servants' pallet she'd been sleeping on, she curled in a ball and cried.

She couldn't tell if she was happy or sad or relieved, but certainly she was at the end of a long and worrisome road. And she was inexpressibly joyful about her future.

As her body shook with tears, she laughed on top of the relief. Who sobs when they have at last found joy? Exhaustion took over though and she found herself nodding off with a smile.

The next morning, Mrs. Gibbons was up and working when Grace walked down the stairs. "Are you well?" She rested a hand on the woman's shoulder.

"Oh yes, my dear. At last, I am well."

Grace tied an apron around herself. "Please take care. Rest when you need to."

"I will, but don't you be worrying about me. It's you

who needs to rest. He's home. It's time you went back to your family." She placed a hand at the side of Grace's face. "As much as we will miss you."

Grace embraced her. "I will miss all of you. And this work."

Mrs. Gibbons just smiled and then moved about the front room. "I think many of our guests are going home this morning. The sickness seems to have traveled through to everyone it's going to take this time."

"What an awful illness."

"It is." She gently pushed Grace toward the kitchen. "Now, get yourself a bite and head on back to your house. Lord Stewart should not be up for hours yet."

"I'm up." He closed his study door and walked toward them, tall, strong, neatly dressed. Grace's insides were immediately aflutter. "And good morning to you."

"Thank you. I slept amazingly well in my study. Perhaps that shall be a second bedroom for me from now on."

Grace laughed. "I was just on my way to get some breakfast. Will you be joining me?"

"I would like that very much." He turned to Mrs. Gibbons. "I am so pleased you are doing well. I heard the servants were worried for a time."

"I weathered through. I'm stronger than I look." She smiled. "It's good to have you home."

"I'm happy to be home. It's simple here but much finer than the dusty old hunting cabin I found."

Mrs. Gibbons gasped. "That's terrible. When I think of all you've done, all you've been through." She brought a handkerchief to her eyes. "I can hardly bear it."

"I bore it just fine and lived to tell the tale, so don't you be concerning yourself overly much. Instead, let's get these fine people well and home to their families." He winked.

"Agreed." His dear housekeeper shuffled away.

Lord Stewart held out his arm. "Might I accompany you to the kitchen? I hear that's where we take our meals now."

"Yes, here in the vicarage, while we have guests, all meals are served in the kitchen." She grinned. "I can give you a tour if you'd like."

"I feel like I'll need one." He rested a hand over the top of hers. "You were a marvel. I don't even know how to thank you."

"There is no need. I felt compelled to do something."

"What brought you here in the first place? How did you discover our predicament?"

She looked down. "That's an interesting story."

"Would you like to tell it over Cook's biscuits?"

"I could, or we could wait until you get yourself settled in at the castle."

"Am I coming there?"

"You have nowhere to sleep here, not really, or even a quiet moment to think. We have rooms to spare."

"As tempting as that offer is, and I would be tempted in more ways than one," he stepped nearer, his wildly wiggling eyebrows were ridiculous enough to make her laugh, "I must stay and finish what you've begun at the vicarage. But I have asked for an audience with Lord Morley this afternoon. Perhaps I might request a turn about your gardens while I'm there. I would appreciate an audience alone with you if I may?" His eyes were full of love and light—as though he could hardly wait to tell her the best secret in the world.

She stared into them, knowing she would never

discover all the secrets they held, but wanting to try, none-theless. At last she answered, "Of course. I will be counting the minutes until I see you again."

"As will I." He pressed his lips to her forehead. "I cannot believe how blessed my life has suddenly become."

"And mine." She shook her head. "I never want to feel lost like that again. I never want to not know where you are." She shook her head and shivered. "But let's talk of other things."

They sat together in the large, thick wood table that usually housed the servants or Cook's cutting board or any number of other projects that caused all the scratches and grooves. Grace loved every bit of it. She had helped assemble many a basket for the poor on that very table. But now she and Lord Stewart put jam on biscuits together as though it were the most normal thing in the world. As if every day could be like that for them. She hardly dared believe it could be.

His eyes danced with daring. "So, are you going to tell me what brought you here?"

"Oh yes." She swallowed and then took a sip of tea. "So we were sitting around our courtyard, every Standish sister at home. It was quite lovely."

"Charity is in town?" He smiled.

"Yes, just for this meeting."

"Oh, so it was the marriage meeting?"

"It was. And they had all decided."

"Ah."

"Yes. Morley sung Lord Featherstone's praises, and everyone seemed to agree. I asked if anyone else had talked to him or come to him to ask for my hand and Morley said no." She lifted accusing eyes to him but then laughed to soften the blow. "And we've already talked about this. But what you didn't know was that I left in that moment and came here."

"You walked out of the room?" He laughed.

"I did. I left them all sitting there while I came to find you."

"And what would you have told me if I was here?"

"Well, I would have marched right in, called your name, and said, "Lord Stewart—"

"Oliver."

"Oh? Oliver. I like that. But back then, I would have said Lord Stewart."

"True, carry on, then."

"Lord Stewart. Why have you not talked to Morley about us? Are you having doubts about whether or not you wish to court me?"

"Excellent question."

"Thank you. I rehearsed it the whole way."

"Very good."

She nodded. "But then you weren't here. And the rest has been one very busy, exhausting time."

He pulled her close again and rested his head on top of hers while they sat. "I am so sorry you had to wonder even for one moment about my sincerity." He shook his head. "If I could, I'd wipe every single worried thought from your memory." His sigh filled the air around them. "As it is, will you please come to me the minute another similar thought ever comes to plague you?"

"Yes, if you'll do the same for me. You have much to do and be concerned over. I'd like to share that burden."

"You will be such a strength to me. I cannot even believe my sudden and extreme good fortune. But let us save the rest of our overflowing of amazement until this afternoon. Will I see you at the castle?"

"You can count on it."

They finished up their simple meal, and Oliver walked Grace to the door and she left.

Her walk home was long, much longer than the walk to the vicarage. She wished for a carriage or a cart or something to rest her tired feet, but there were none to spare at the vicarage. At last she arrived at the castle. Someone must have seen her coming because all of her sisters were just inside the door when she opened it.

She laughed and then fell into their arms.

"Oh, Grace, was it so hard?" Kate hugged her tight.

"It was, but it was glorious as well. The food from the castle was a godsend. Your blankets and supplies . . . I couldn't have done any of it without you all." She reached for two of her sisters' hands. "Why must we all live apart? It is so much better when each of you is here."

Kate and Lucy and Charity smiled back with the love felt between sisters, the love Grace knew would always be there. The kind of love that spoke honestly and with passion about things most cared for.

"Let's go sit with June. I have news!" Grace nearly squealed her news as they all rushed up the stairs. "June!" Grace called to her. "She's awake, isn't she?" She put a hand over her mouth, hoping she hadn't just woken her sister.

June sat at a chair near her window. Her face lit when Grace walked into the room.

"I'm so pleased you're back. Tell me all about it."

206

"I have the best, most wonderful news. You will all be quite amazed."

They climbed up onto June's bed as they had all done through their lives. Kate started a braid in Grace's hair out of habit. Grace toyed with the ribbons on Lucy's dress. June sat carefully, her full belly a difficult thing to find comfortable, apparently. And Charity tucked her feet underneath her with hands in her lap. She smiled at them all. "I'm so happy to be back."

They laughed together and then all eyes turned to Grace.

"I'm going to be married!" She laughed.

Everyone nodded. "Yes, we know."

"No, not to Lord Featherstone."

June gasped. "What do you mean? I think Morley's already talked to him."

Grace waved excited hands in the air. "I know all that. And Charles is perfectly alright with the new plan."

"Who, Morley? He should have told me." June frowned.

"No, Lord Featherstone." She waved her hands. "This afternoon Lord Stewart has asked for an audience with Morley." She clasped her hands together and sat up on her knees, waiting for their reaction.

Which was slow in coming.

Grace looked from one sister to the next. "Are you not so pleased? I've made a choice. I want to marry Lord Stewart, and I'm to be the happiest of you all, for we are most powerfully in love!" She laughed.

But they looked concerned.

"Sisters." She looked from one to the other again, a feather of concern growing. "Come celebrate with me."

"Lord Stewart?" Kate nodded. "Not Lord Featherstone, his brother?"

"No, he's lovely, of course, but I don't love him."

"I thought you were not interested in love. I thought you wanted us to choose so that you could make the most logical choice . . ." Lucy crossed her legs, adjusting her skirts.

"I know I said that, but it was before I knew what it felt like to fall in love. I would do anything for him, go anywhere. I don't care what his situation is, I want to be with him. Surely you understand this, Lucy."

She nodded. "I do, of course. We all had love matches."

"Then, what is the problem here?"

"We want to know if he makes sense in your head as well as your heart." June waved her over. "Come sit by me, love. We are happy for you, but you asked us here to make certain you do what is best for you."

Grace nodded. "I suppose I did."

Charity leaned back against the headboard and pulled her skirts to her ankles. "It all boils down to one question."

"And what is that?" Grace looked from one serious face to another, growing more concerned by the minute.

The sisters' faces suddenly changed from serious to overly pleased, then Kate jumped up. "What are we all going to wear to the wedding?" She laughed and danced on the bed.

The others joined her, all except June, in a bouncing, giggling mass.

"Oh, come, June. At least stand with us." Charity reached down to help her up. It took two other sisters to pull her to her feet, but soon they were all hugging and bouncing together on the bed.

June laughed. "To think, there was a time I wasn't certain any of us would marry, and now look. Each one as happy as the next." She wiped at her tears. "This might be the best day of my life."

Suddenly water ran down her legs and she doubled over in pain, clutching her stomach. "The baby is coming." She gasped. "Get Morley and the doctor."

Charity lowered her to a sitting position on the bed and stayed with her, but the rest of the sisters ran from the room, screaming for Morley and Mrs. Pinkel, the midwife, and for Dr. Green. No one in the house or the nearby buildings was left with any doubt that Lady Morley was about to deliver.

CHAPTER 22

*O*liver dressed with extra care. His cravat was a new style. His jacket was crisp. His boots were shined. His hair was perfectly placed. He was newly shaven. He even placed a hint of orange-sandalwood-smelling waters at the base of his neck and ran mint-flavored sticks over his teeth. He was everything he used to be in his early days of attending Seasons *and* everything he had become as he'd tried to love and serve a congregation these past few years. Lord Stewart was off to propose. He kicked up his heels. "Now it's time."

"Yes, m'lord." His valet eyed him. "You are ready."

"I am ready." Oliver smiled.

He stepped out of his room, where all three of his brothers waited. George whistled. "There's the Oliver we know and love."

"Very nice, brother." Jacob clucked his tongue.

Then Charles clapped him on the back. "Do you know what you're going to say?"

"I think I'll just ask her to marry me."

"Of course, but have you planned out the exact words?"

"No, I hoped I could just feel in the moment and go with whatever came."

Charles's mouth dropped. "Oh heavens, no, do not do that." He handed him some scrawled words on a piece of paper. "I've pretended to be you for an hour. It was not my best moment, but I thought of some words you can use. Organize them however you like so they're yours. But you might want to glance over the list on your way to the castle."

"Thank you." He rested a hand on Charles's shoulder. "And thank you for what you did to bring us together."

"It was my best job. Didn't get paid one penny for it, but I've never been more proud of my work here." He smiled. "Now, go seal the deal so I don't have to spend one more second in this hovel."

"We all know you're staying until the end of the Season."

"Too true. But I have a client arriving tomorrow, a legitimate, paying one, and that should get us back to London before we know it."

"Excellent. I'm off. If anyone stops by looking for the vicar, tell them to come back another day."

Charles lifted his hand in the air with a swirl. "I could try my hand at religious counseling . . ."

Oliver turned to him. "Don't you dare."

He held up his hands. "Just offering. Some of these women are pathetically desperate and could use some genuine help with the way they think."

Oliver turned on his path down the hallway. "On

second thought, counsel with as many of the women as you'd like."

Charles's grin grew. "Most excellent."

Oliver climbed into his carriage which he noticed had been newly shined. Charles' doing no doubt.

But when he pulled up to the front of the castle, nothing was as he expected. Dr. Green went running in through the front door, which was left open behind him.

Oliver's heart pounded. "No." He tore out of his carriage and went flying into the house.

Servants were running everywhere. He was nearly trampled by a maid carrying a stack of linens and then another with a bucket of steaming water.

"What is happening?" He called out to anyone who might be listening, but apparently no one was.

Upstairs, a door opened and then shut.

He stepped into the courtyard to hopefully get a better view of things, a suspicion easing his worries.

Kate ran down the hall, calling, "She's asking for Morley, where is that brother of ours?"

Another voice shouted, "Has anyone heard from Gerald? He and Amelia wished to be here!"

Oliver had no idea who that is. Perhaps the duke they talk so much of.

Then Grace stepped out of a door. She had the largest smile and a glow on her cheeks that confirmed his happiest suspicions. She paused a moment at the banister and looked out across the way.

"Grace." His voice was low, but she turned to him immediately, her lovely hair falling all down around her shoulders.

"Oliver."

"Is Lady Morley having a baby?"

"She is. And we're all so excited."

"What can I do?" He grinned up into her lovely face—his angel, Grace.

"You can just stand there and look handsome for a moment. You're all I need right now."

"I can do that." He brought a hand to his chin.

Grace laughed, a musical sound that filled the whole courtyard.

Then Morley raced up the stairs, taking at least three at a time. "Where is she?"

Grace turned. "She's in her room. She's calling for you. And she's doing great."

Morley stopped to hug Grace and noticed Oliver standing where he was.

"Oh, Lord Stewart. You've come to talk about Grace. It's completely up to her. She is going to make all her own marriage decisions from now on. I give my hearty consent to whatever she tells me."

"Most excellent," Oliver called up.

"Welcome to the family." Morley waved and then stopped in front of June's door. He took a full breath, closed his eyes and stepped into the room, closing the door behind him.

Oliver felt his own eyes grow misty. "Are you going to come down here so I can talk to you properly?"

"I don't know. I like this position." She laughed. "You could sing to me."

"I could. But I don't know how much good that would

do at convincing you to spend your life with me. It might potentially do quite the opposite."

She began a slow walk along the banister toward the stairs. "Spend my life with you? That seems like a huge commitment."

"It is, the hugest of them all. I could ask you to shorten it, start with a month or two, perhaps?"

Her steps slowed. "That doesn't sound very appropriate to me."

"Oh, it would be devilishly terrible." His hand rested on the railing, resisting the urge to run up the stairs to meet her.

"Then perhaps we should stay with the lifetime plan."

"I tend to agree. That was the plan I decided upon leaving my house." He held out his hand.

"And can you guarantee grand happiness and a life without care?"

"I'm afraid I cannot."

"Can you promise me lavish houses and trips to the Continent?"

"I cannot."

"How about a house full of children?"

"I cannot even promise that."

She arrived in front of him and took his hand. "Then, Oliver, what can you promise?" Her eyes sparkled; her full mouth smiled.

He tucked that precious hand in his arm, and they began a slow walk toward the side door but she shook her head. "No. Come this way."

She led him down a narrow walkway, to an even more narrow, circular stair. "Have you seen the top of the turret?"

"I have not. Intriguing."

"Yes, it is a grand adventure in my own house."

"Ah, and you love grand adventures."

"I do, but they have to stay close to home."

He laughed. "The best kind."

She led him up stair after stair, sticking as close to him as was possible while walking until they at last stepped out onto a flat area, all of Brighton opening out in every direction. The wind blew, but not overly so. And Oliver found the spot perfect for what he was about to do.

"What do you think?" She spun in a circle with her hands out.

"I am completely enchanted." He pulled her into his arms and began the most scandalous waltz of his life, their bodies close, moving together as one. "This is even more marvelous." He stared into her face, wanting to drink in every feature, every movement of her eyes, her lips. "I love you, Miss Grace Standish."

"And I love you." Her breathless response made him smile. His heart hummed with happiness.

He reached inside his inner pocket and brought out a ring. "I have something I've been longing to ask you."

Her eyes filled with tears. "I long to hear it."

He dropped to one knee and took her hand in his. "Marry me. Join our love as one, be mine in everything as I am yours. Forever."

Her eyes shone back at him, and she lowered to kneel with him. With a hand at the side of his face, she nodded, tears welling and then falling gently. "I will marry you and love you forever. We shall be the happiest of any couple anywhere." Her tender eyes looked deeply into his, showing him all the promise of a happy life. Then she ran her fingers lightly over his mouth, studying it as intently as anything before he groaned in his urgent need to capture those fingers one by one, then her lips. He stood, pulling her into his arms, holding her as close as he could and then covered her mouth with his own.

She gripped him, her fingers digging into the back of his neck with an urgency and power that he could only match with his own.

He cradled her and loved her and ran hungry lips over hers again and again, his heart pounding with hers, commanding the union, celebrating their love.

Time passed unnoticed, but he slowed his kisses and caught his breath as he tugged at her mouth softly, slowly, one lip at a time, glorying in the beauty that was Grace.

"I've never felt this way," he breathed.

"Hmm." She smiled. "Can we do that again?"

His chuckle was deep and low, and he could only grin. "Every day."

"Then let's begin right now." She kissed him again and he responded right where they left off, slowly, intently exploring her mouth until the world spun around him.

A maid burst out onto the turret with them and then turned around. "Forgive me, Miss Grace, but Lady Morley..."

Grace turned, still in his arms. "Is everything all right?"

"Yes, it's perfectly lovely. They're asking for you. The baby is here, miss." The maid curtseyed and ran back down the stairs.

Grace laughed. "Oh, we must meet her at once." She

grabbed hold of his hand like she would never let go and tugged him to follow her back down the stairs.

"Do you know it will be a girl, then?"

"Of course! She's a Standish, after all."

EPILOGUE

*L*ord Featherstone watched another wedding. These things were the longest ceremonies of all creation. Every time he wondered why the thing could not be shortened somehow. All the words and the ritual dragged on and on. He resisted the urge to check his watch fob. This particular wedding, although long, was his greatest happiness, perhaps until his own.

His younger brother Oliver and Miss Grace Standish stood together, and by the looks of them, they didn't care one whit that they'd all been sitting there watching for over two hours.

He laughed to himself and was promptly shushed by someone, a matron somewhere, no doubt.

But a woman, a young woman, turned to him, her bright green eyes brilliant in the dim light of the church. Her raised eyebrow and slight look of amused disapproval intrigued him. But he let her see only the hint of his intrigue. It did not do to play lapdog at first glance to a beautiful woman. One must convince her slowly that they were the only man who could ever see her deepest core, the only man who could love her as she deserved to be loved. As he eyed her, it was his first opinion that she wished to be loved deeply, passionately, and emotionally. He shifted in his pew. He might not be ready for that kind of love.

But she'd done it. She was under his skin.

The question now remained. When would he do something about it?

* * *

Weeks later, Oliver stood at the front of his congregation, his wife sat just below him on their family pew. He couldn't help but look there again and again. Some day, that pew would hold their children, their grandchildren. Across from her sat the Standish sisters and their families. They now filled two pews when everyone came.

And at the highest spot in the room, the royal box, sat Prince George.

The chapel was packed.

Oliver was about to give the sermon of his life. It was bold. It was daring. But it was needed. After looking at each member of the congregation in turn, and with another glance at Grace, he began. "Today I would like to talk to you all about one of the best, most blessed commandments of all time. We find it in Genesis, in the beginning. '. . . a man shall cleave unto his wife and they shall be one flesh.'"

The prince's face beamed with happiness as he leaned forward in his seat. Lord Featherstone laughed out loud in pure enjoyment. A few gasps followed, but Oliver continued on.

One flesh. He and Grace were working on it, more every day, in more ways than one.

And though they'd had their arguments already, mostly caused by his own inadequacies, they were committed to each other and to their family. As they also raised their eyes to heaven, it would be a glorious life indeed.

The End.

To read more of Lord Featherstone, pre-order his first book HERE.

FOLLOW JEN

Follow her Newsletter

To read more of Lord Featherstone, Pre-order his first book HERE

Some of Jen's other published books

The Nobleman's Daughter
Two lovers in disguise

Scarlet
The Pimpernel retold

A Lady's Maid
Can she love again?

His Lady in Hiding
Hiding out at his maid.

Spun of Gold
Rumpelstilskin Retold

Dating the Duke
Time Travel: Regency man in NYC

Charmed by His Lordship
The antics of a fake friendship

Tabitha's Folly
Four over-protective Brothers

To read Damen's Secret
The Villain's Romance

TO WIN HER HAND

Have you ever met a man with a certain air who understands the female mind? He knows what to say, how to dress, and what to do to win her over? Or at least, he thinks he does. Order HERE or on Amazon.

That man is Lord Featherstone.

In a desperate move to earn more money and save his estate, he turns his talents into a business venture and becomes London's biggest and most sought after secret matchmaker...for men.

LORDS FOR THE SISTERS OF SUSSEX

The Duke's Second Chance
 The Earl's Winning Wager
 Her Lady's Whims and Whimsies
 Suitors for the Proper Miss
 Pining for Lord Lockhart
 The Foibles and Follies of Miss Grace

Follow Jen's Newsletter for a free book and to stay up to date on her releases. https://www.subscribepage.com/y8p6z9

Made in the USA
Columbia, SC
24 March 2022